W9-CKI-594

Modern Critical Interpretations

Alexander Pope's

The Rape of the Lock

Modern Critical Interpretations

The Oresteia
Beowulf
The General Prologue to The Canterbury Tales
The Pardoner's Tale
The Knight's Tale
The Divine Comedy
Exodus
Genesis
The Gospels
The Iliad
The Book of Job
Volpone
Doctor Faustus
The Revelation of St. John the Divine
The Song of Songs
Oedipus Rex
The Aeneid
The Duchess of Malfi
Antony and Cleopatra
As You Like It
Coriolanus
Hamlet
Henry IV, Part I
Henry IV, Part II
Henry V
Julius Caesar
King Lear
Macbeth
Measure for Measure
The Merchant of Venice
A Midsummer Night's Dream
Much Ado About Nothing
Othello
Richard II
Richard III
The Sonnets
Taming of the Shrew
The Tempest
Twelfth Night
The Winter's Tale
Emma
Mansfield Park
Pride and Prejudice
The Life of Samuel Johnson
Moll Flanders
Robinson Crusoe
Tom Jones
The Beggar's Opera
Gray's Elegy
Paradise Lost
The Rape of the Lock
Tristram Shandy
Gulliver's Travels
Evelina
The Marriage of Heaven and Hell
Songs of Innocence and Experience
Jane Eyre
Wuthering Heights
Don Juan
The Rime of the Ancient Mariner
Bleak House
David Copperfield
Hard Times
A Tale of Two Cities
Middlemarch
The Mill on the Floss
Jude the Obscure
The Mayor of Casterbridge
The Return of the Native
Tess of the D'Urbervilles
The Odes of Keats
Frankenstein
Vanity Fair
Barchester Towers
The Prelude
The Red Badge of Courage
The Scarlet Letter
The Ambassadors
Daisy Miller, The Turn of the Screw, and Other Tales
The Portrait of a Lady
Billy Budd, Benito Cereno, Bartleby the Scrivener, and Other Tales
Moby-Dick
The Tales of Poe
Walden
Adventures of Huckleberry Finn
The Life of Frederick Douglass
Heart of Darkness
Lord Jim
Nostromo
A Passage to India
Dubliners
A Portrait of the Artist as a Young Man
Ulysses
Kim
The Rainbow
Sons and Lovers
Women in Love
1984
Major Barbara
Man and Superman
Pygmalion
St. Joan
The Playboy of the Western World
The Importance of Being Earnest
Mrs. Dalloway
To the Lighthouse
My Antonia
An American Tragedy
Murder in the Cathedral
The Waste Land
Absalom, Absalom!
Light in August
Sanctuary
The Sound and the Fury
The Great Gatsby
A Farewell to Arms
The Sun Also Rises
Arrowsmith
Lolita
The Iceman Cometh
Long Day's Journey Into Night
The Grapes of Wrath
Miss Lonelyhearts
The Glass Menagerie
A Streetcar Named Desire
Their Eyes Were Watching God
Native Son
Waiting for Godot
Herzog
All My Sons
Death of a Salesman
Gravity's Rainbow
All the King's Men
The Left Hand of Darkness
The Brothers Karamazov
Crime and Punishment
Madame Bovary
The Interpretation of Dreams
The Castle
The Metamorphosis
The Trial
Man's Fate
The Magic Mountain
Montaigne's Essays
Remembrance of Things Past
The Red and the Black
Anna Karenina
War and Peace

These and other titles in preparation

Modern Critical Interpretations

Alexander Pope's
The Rape of the Lock

Edited and with an introduction by
Harold Bloom
Sterling Professor of the Humanities
Yale University

Chelsea House Publishers ◇ 1988
NEW YORK ◇ NEW HAVEN ◇ PHILADELPHIA

Printed and bound in the United States of America

10 9 8 7 6 5 4 3 2 1

∞ The paper used in this publication meets the minimum requirements of the American National Standard for Permanence of Paper for Printed Library Materials, Z39.48-1984.

Library of Congress Cataloging-in-Publication Data
Alexander Pope's The rape of the lock.
(Modern critical interpretations)
Bibliography: p.
Includes index.
1. Pope, Alexander, 1688–1744. Rape of the lock.
I. Bloom, Harold. II. Series.
PR3629.A78 1988 821′.5 87-25607
ISBN 0–87754–422–0 (alk. paper)

Contents

Editor's Note

This book brings together a representative selection of the best modern critical interpretations of Alexander Pope's mock-heroic satire, *The Rape of the Lock*. The critical essays are reprinted here in the chronological order of their original publication. I am grateful to Christina Büchmann for her assistance in editing this volume.

My introduction considers the problematic relation between heroic and mock-heroic in Pope's *Rape of the Lock*. Martin Price begins the chronological sequence of criticism with an incisive statement of the way in which the "double vision" of the mock-heroic scale can suggest manners merging into morals. Emrys Jones, also meditating upon the mock-heroic, examines its appeal to some of the greatest creative minds of the century.

William K. Wimsatt, most heroic of Popeans, brilliantly expounds the poem's fascinating employment of the game of ombre. In Robin Grove's overview, *The Rape of the Lock* ultimately is seen as a hymn that celebrates mutability itself.

Social history is the focus of C. E. Nicholson's essay, while K. M. Quinsey centers upon the extraordinary range manifested by the satire in the poem. David Fairer sets *The Rape of the Lock*'s dialectics of truth and imagination in the British empiricist tradition. This volume concludes with A. C. Büchmann's brief but illuminating essay on Pope's miniaturist artistry in the poem.

Introduction

> *The character of* Belinda, *as we take it in this third View, represents the Popish Religion, or the Whore of* Babylon; *who is described in the state this malevolent Author wishes for, coming forth in all her Glory upon the* Thames, *and overspreading the Nation with Ceremonies.*
>
> *A Key to the Lock*

In April 1715, writing under the splendid name of Esdras Barnikelt, apothecary, Pope published *A Key to the Lock,* with the subtitle "Or a Treatise proving, beyond all Contradiction, the dangerous Tendency of a late Poem entitled *The Rape of the Lock* to Government and Religion." The continued use of the *Key* is to warn critics not to seek a key to Pope's mock-epic, which is to say, do not apply critical "methods" to one of the most poised and artful poems in Western literature.

Critics long have recognized that the genres of epic and mock-epic are not clearly distinct in or for Pope. *The Rape of the Lock* participates in the heroic mode rather more subtly than Pope's Homer does. The most surprising assertion as to this is the judgment of Reuben Brower:

> By inventing the sylphs Pope solved the almost impossible problems that the theorists set for the heroic poet. He is almost certainly the only modern poet to create a company of believable deities which are not simply the ancient classical divinities in modern dress, and which are not offensive to a Christian audience.

What makes Brower's remarks problematical centers in the phrase "offensive to a Christian audience," though "*believable* deities" also perhaps begs the question. Milton's angels remain Milton's, and the deities of late Shakespearean romance are persuasive (if not "believable") and offensive to no one. This is to cite only the greatest; examples are too profuse to be catalogued. Brower's true point, I think, was that Pope brilliantly exploited the shadowy ground between heroic and mock-heroic poetry. The play of allusions, splendidly studied by Brower, seems to me unlike the two fundamental modes set forth by John Hollander. Pope is neither like Donne and his Modernist followers, who give us a sense that baroque elaboration of metaphor is almost infinitely possible, nor is Pope like Milton and his Romantic followers, including such twentieth-century Romantics as W. B. Yeats and Wallace Stevens, who so station their allusions as to make further figuration almost redundant. In his own mode of refinement, Pope lightly but strongly intimates that more turnings of allusion always are possible, while charmingly insinuating that the elegance and justice of his tropes will constitute a proper haven for the amiable reader.

Martin Price calls *The Rape of the Lock* "the heroic-turned-artful." Belinda's world, on the epic scale, is second-best, even trivial, but "it is also a world of grace and delicacy." Charm replaces heroic action, a substitution principally symbolized by the Rosicrucian machinery of the sylphs:

> The principal symbol of the triviality of Belinda's world is the machinery of sylphs and gnomes. The "light militia of the lower sky" are a travesty of both Homeric deities and Miltonic guardian angels. Like their originals, they have an ambiguous status: they exist within and without the characters. They are, in their diminutive operation, like those small but constant self-regarding gestures we may associate with a lady conscious of her charms. The sylphs who protect Belinda are also her acceptance of the rules of social convention, which presume that a coquette's life is pure game. The central action of the poem is Belinda's descent from coquette to prude, from the dazzling rival of the sun ("Belinda smil'd, and all the world was gay") to the rancorous Amazon who shrieks in self-righteous anger. It is Clarissa who vainly points to the loss. Her speech in the last canto is a parody, as Pope reminds us, of Sarpedon's speech to Glaucus in book XII of the *Iliad*. For "the utter generosity of spirit, the supreme magnanimity of attitude" with which Sarpedon faces the loss of life, Clarissa offers to Belinda a substitute that is analogous: within the scale of the playground world of the coquette there is the selflessness of "good humor," the ability to place value rightly and accept the conditions of life. This will permit Belinda to retain the radiance that has warmed and illumined her world.

The only modification I would suggest to Price's superb observations is that the sylphs dialectically both travesty and yet surpass (in a knowingly limited but crucial way) the Homeric gods and the Miltonic angels, partly by shrewdly compounding both with the Shakespearean fairies, and with the specifically Ovidian elements in *A Midsummer Night's Dream*. Homer and Milton perhaps are not so much travestied by Pope as they are Shakespeareanized and Ovidianized. Instead of the sagacious Athena and the affable Archangel Raphael, we are given the sylphs who are Ovidian sophisticated flirts. Their sophistication is keen enough to be poetically dangerous. Let us take, as instance, the most flamboyant parody of the sacred Milton in Pope's poem:

> But when to Mischief Mortals bend their Will,
> How soon they find fit Instruments of Ill!
> Just then, *Clarissa* drew with tempting Grace
> A two-edg'd Weapon from her shining Case;
> So Ladies in Romance assist their Knight,
> Present the Spear, and arm him for the Fight.
> He takes the Gift with rev'rence, and extends
> The little Engine on his Fingers' Ends,
> This just behind *Belinda's* Neck he spread,
> As o'er the fragrant Steams she bends her Head:
> Swift to the Lock a thousand Sprights repair,
> A thousand Wings, by turns, blow back the Hair,
> And thrice they twitch'd the Diamond in her Ear,
> Thrice she look'd back, and thrice the Foe drew near.
> Just in that instant, anxious *Ariel* sought
> The close Recesses of the Virgin's Thought;
> As on the Nosegay in her Breast reclin'd,
> He watch'd th' Ideas rising in her Mind,
> Sudden he view'd in spite of all her Art,
> An Earthly Lover lurking at her Heart.
> Amaz'd, confus'd, he found his Pow'r expir'd,
> Resign'd to Fate, and with a Sigh retir'd.
> The Peer now spreads the glitt'ring *Forfex* wide,
> T'inclose the Lock; now joins it, to divide.
> Ev'n then, before the fatal Engine clos'd,
> A wretched *Sylph* too fondly interpos'd;
> Fate urg'd the Sheers, and cut the *Sylph* in twain,
> (But Airy Substance soon unites again)

The meeting Points the sacred Hair dissever
From the fair Head, for ever and for ever!

That "wretched *Sylph*," as Pope's own note tells us, is suggested by the Miltonic blunder "of Satan cut asunder by the Angel Michael":

but the sword
Of Michael from the armoury of God
Was given him tempered so, that neither keen
Nor solid might resist that edge: it met
The sword of Satan with steep force to smite
Descending, and in half cut sheer, nor stayed,
But with swift wheel reverse, deep entering shared
All his right side; then Satan first knew pain,
And writhed him to and fro convolved; so sore
The griding sword with discontinuous wound
Passed through him, but the ethereal substance closed
Not long divisible, and from the gash
A stream of nectarous humour issuing flowed
Sanguine, such as celestial spirits may bleed,
And all his armour stained ere while so bright.
Forthwith on all sides to his aid was run
By angels many and strong who interposed
Defence, while others bore him on their shields
Back to his chariot; where it stood retired
From off the files of war; there they him laid
Gnashing for anguish and despite and shame
To find himself not matchless, and his pride
Humbled by such rebuke, so far beneath
His confidence to equal God in power.
Yet soon he healed; for spirits that live throughout
Vital in every part, not as frail man
In entrails, heart or head, liver or reins,
Cannot but by annihilating die;
Nor in their liquid texture mortal wound
Receive, no more than can the fluid air:
All heart they live, all head, all eye, all ear,
All intellect, all sense, and as they please,
They limb themselves, and colour, shape or size
Assume, as likes them best, condense or rare.

A comparison of the two passages will demonstrate Pope's triumph over the sublimely humorless Milton, who for once works entirely too hard to transume Homer and Virgil and Spenser. Michael's sword transcends the blade given by Astraea to Arthegall in book 5 of *The Faerie Queene,* where it would pierce and cleave whatever came against it. More overtly, the Miltonic sword (out of the prophet Jeremiah's armory of God) greatly outdoes the armor of Aeneas, against which the sword of Turnus shattered into chunks. Satan is dreadfully chopped up, and like the Homeric gods, he can be wounded, and suffer pain, but he cannot be killed. Yet Homer's Ares, wounded in battle, is fiercely impressive, while not just Satan but the poet Milton loses dignity when we read "Yet soon he healed . . . ," because he is of those spirits: "Nor in their liquid texture mortal wound / Receive, no more than can the fluid air."

Pope rather wickedly overgoes Milton by turning the entire cumbersome Satanic passage into one airy, parenthetical line, the superb throwaway of "(But Airy Substance soon unites again)," strikingly contrasted to the Ovidian mock-pathos of the couplet following. The fond Sylph and proud Satan soon heal, but Belinda's lock and Belinda's fair head are forever separated:

> The meeting Points the sacred Hair dissever From the fair Head,
> for ever and for ever!

Outrageously moved as we are by "for ever and for ever," we are compelled to award the palm to Pope over Milton, in this instance. The greatness of *The Rape of the Lock* is that it may be the only poem that seems to demand Mozartean comparisons, because it too is infinitely nuanced, absolutely controlled, and yet finally poignant in the highest degree.

Patterns of Civility: Art and Morality

Martin Price

In *The Rape of the Lock* we move from the nature-become-art of the pastoral to the heroic-turned-artful. The world of Belinda is a world of triviality measured against the epic scale; it is also a world of grace and delicacy, a second-best world but not at all a contemptible one. Here Pope has built upon a theme that plays against the epic tradition: the mock-heroic world (in Dryden's version) of Virgil's bees is a world that has some real, if extravagant, claim to the epic style. The *Georgics* celebrate a mundane heroism and place it against the special virtues of the martial hero.

The emphasis of the epic had, moreover, moved by Pope's day—through Spenser and Milton—further and further toward spiritual conflict. In *The Rape of the Lock* the primary quality of Belinda is spiritual shallowness, an incapacity for moral awareness. She has transformed all spiritual exercises and emblems into a coquette's self-display and self-adoration. All of it is done with a frivolous heedlessness; she is not quite a hypocrite.

> Fair nymphs, and well-drest youths around her shone,
> But ev'ry eye was fix'd on her alone.
> On her white breast a sparkling cross she wore,
> Which Jews might kiss, and Infidels adore.
>
> (2.5–8)

Our perspective closes more and more sharply, upon Belinda as cynosure, and upon the sparkling cross that fixes attention upon her beauty. The cross

From *To the Palace of Wisdom: Studies in Order and Energy from Dryden to Blake.*

is a religious symbol turned to the uses of ornament, and by the rules of the little world of the poem it gains new power through this translation. At every point in the poem grace and charm supplant depth of feeling or heroic action; the only direct survivors of the old heroic virtues are the miniature playing cards. Here Pope's play with scale becomes most fascinating. Within the heroic frame of the mock-epic language we have the miniature world of belles and beaux, who live by an elaborate and formal set of rules. Within that small world is framed in turn the card game (with its further formalization of rules), where kings and queens, mortal battles and shameful seductions, still survive, as a game within a game.

The principal symbol of the triviality of Belinda's world is the machinery of sylphs and gnomes. The "light militia of the lower sky" are a travesty of both Homeric deities and Miltonic guardian angels. Like their originals, they have an ambiguous status: they exist within and without the characters. They are, in their diminutive operation, like those small but constant self-regarding gestures we may associate with a lady conscious of her charms. The sylphs who protect Belinda are also her acceptance of the rules of social convention, which presume that a coquette's life is pure game. The central action of the poem is Belinda's descent from coquette to prude, from the dazzling rival of the sun ("Belinda smil'd, and all the world was gay") to the rancorous Amazon who shrieks in self-righteous anger. It is Clarissa who vainly points to the loss. Her speech in the last canto is a parody, as Pope reminds us, of Sarpedon's speech to Glaucus in book 12 of the *Iliad*. For "the utter generosity of spirit, the supreme magnanimity of attitude" with which Sarpedon faces the loss of life, Clarissa offers to Belinda a substitute that is analogous: within the scale of the playground world of the coquette there is the selflessness of "good humor," the ability to place value rightly and accept the conditions of life. This will permit Belinda to retain the radiance that has warmed and illumined her world.

Pope's use of scale has set up a double view of this playworld. It has the smallness of scale and fineness of organization of the work of art, yet like a game, it is temporary and threatens to break down. "At any moment 'ordinary life' may reassert its rights either by an impact from without, which interrupts the game, or by an offense against the rules, or else from within, by a collapse of the play spirit, a sobering, a disenchantment." Clarissa's speech offers a view of life as it must be when the playing has to stop. Thalestris offers the outrage of the spoilsport. "By withdrawing from the game [the spoilsport] reveals the relativity and fragility of the playworld in which he had temporarily shut himself with others. He robs play of its *illusion*—a pregnant word which means literally 'in-play' (from *inlusio, illudere,* or *inludere*)." Pope's play-world in *The Rape of the Lock* hovers between the trivial fragility of mere play (with its obliviousness to the possibilities of mature life) and the preciousness of a life ordered with grace, however minute its scale or limited its values.

In the dressing-table scene at the close of canto 1 we see Belinda's beauty both as a mere ornamentation governed by pride and as the realization of a genuine aesthetic ordering. The worship before the mirror of the "cosmetic powers" produces the appearance Belinda wishes to have and which she further adorns, her maid attending "the sacred rites of Pride." With that word, the world pours in, diminished in scale:

> Unnumber'd treasures ope at once, and here
> The various off'rings of the world appear
> . . . .
> This casket India's glowing gems unlocks,
> And all Arabia breathes from yonder box.
> The tortoise here and elephant unite,
> Transform'd to combs, the speckled and the white.
> (ll. 129–30, 133–36)

The spacious world can enter Belinda's dressing room only in a serviceable and diminished form. Arabia is compressed into its perfume; the unwieldy elephant and tortoise are transformed into the elegance of shell and ivory combs. The universe, the Indian philosopher tells us, is a great elephant standing on the back of a tortoise. John Locke had made much of the fable in his treatment of substance. This condensation of the vast into the small is at once reversed: the pins extend into "shining rows" or "files" of soldiers, and Belinda becomes the epic hero investing himself in armor as well as the godlike "awful Beauty." Here is the triumph of art: Belinda "calls forth all the wonders of her face" and gives them realization with her cosmetic skill. She is the mistress of the "bidden blush" but also the culmination of nature. Her art trembles on the precipice of mere artifice, but it retains its poise.

We can say, then, that the world of Belinda is once more a pastoral world, the world of the "town-eclogue." But it is filled with omens: balanced against Belinda's rites of pride are the Baron's prayers at another altar; balanced against Belinda's generous smiles are the labyrinths of her hair. As she descends the Thames, the "painted vessel" is the literal craft on which she sails and also Belinda herself—perhaps reminiscent of the "stately Ship / Of Tarsus . . . With all her bravery on, and tackle trim, /

Sails filled, and streamers waving, / Courted by all the winds that hold them play"—the Dalila of Milton's *Samson Agonistes*. Belinda is at once the pastoral mistress ("Where'er you walk, cool gales shall fan the glade"), the power of harmony, and the imminent temptress and sower of discord. But her greatest power arises from the fact that she is not really aware of what she is leading the Baron to do or of what disaster may befall herself. Like Eve's, her very weakness increases her power for destruction, and the sylphs, lovely but variable, express her ambiguous self-consciousness—the sense of disaster that is also a sense of her power to call forth violence.

With the fall of her coquette's world, as the Baron snips her lock, we descend to the realm of anarchy, and the Cave of Spleen, with its surrealistic atmosphere of fantasy and compulsions. Spleen is the antigoddess; as Dulness is opposed to Light, so here the vindictive and self-pitying passions are opposed to good humor and good sense. This is surely one of the great cave or underworld passages, and we must call to mind the caves of Error and Despair or the dwelling of Night in Spenser to see its full value. Pope's special contribution is closer to the late medieval landscapes of Hieronymus Bosch: an erotic nightmare of exploding libidinous drives. The passions repressed by prudes find neurotic expression in mincing languor or prurient reproach; they scrawl, as it were, those graffiti that are a nasty travesty of love. The Cave of spleen is one of the strongest pictures of disorder in the age: it gives us the measure of order, a sense of the strength of the forces that social decorum controls and of the savage distortion of feeling that it prevents.

The first effect of the entrance of Spleen into the upper world is Thalestris's skeptical questioning of the art Belinda has lavished upon herself:

> Was it for this you took such constant care
> The bodkin, comb, and essence to prepare?
> For this your locks in paper-durance bound,
> For this with tort'ring irons wreath'd around?
>
> (4.97–100)

If we compare these harsh lines with the reverential rites of pride, we can see how false are the doubts cast upon the art of the dressing table under the strain of injured pride. The creative skill that brought nature to its full realization becomes for the prude and spoilsport a torturing of nature by a strained and cruel art. And Belinda herself becomes, in turn, like Lady Wishfort and Mrs. Marwood in Congreve's *The Way of the World*, or even Alceste in Molière's *The Misanthrope*, an affected and pharisaical "primitivist":

> Oh had I rather unadmir'd remain'd
> In some lone isle, or distant northern land
> . . . .
> There kept my charms conceal'd from mortal eye,
> Like roses, that in deserts bloom and die.
> (4.153–54, 157–58)

Belinda is not unmindful of the fragrance she might have wasted, but she is professedly ready to renounce the whole game.

The game is, of course, in her world everything; we need not be put off by an effusion like, "O had I stay'd, and said my pray'rs at home!" (4.160). What Belinda renounces and seeks to destroy, in her spleen, is the pattern of order by which she has lived and of which she was the moving force. It is always someone like Belinda who gives style and grace to a social pattern. If the heroic overtones of the poem constantly insist upon the comparative triviality of this pattern, they serve also to glorify it. Just as the brilliant detail of the Flemish painters gave a heightened reality to those bourgeois subjects that preempted the space of the saints, so Pope's almost dazzling particularity—in each case woven out of generalities of heroic splendor—insists upon the intense if miniature order of his society. The heroic virtues are transposed to the scale of charm, and one cannot resist quoting Burke's famous phrases about another such order:

> It is gone, that sensibility of principle, that chastity of honor, which felt a stain like a wound, which inspired courage whilst it mitigated ferocity, which ennobled whatever it touched, and under which vice itself lost half its evil, by losing all its grossness.
> (*Reflections on the French Revolution,* 1790)

These words define what a code of civilized life must do. *The Rape of the Lock* leaves its moral judgments implicit in its double mock-heroic scale, but it makes of that scale an illuminating vision of art as a sustaining pattern of order. It is an art of "good humor," of tact and charm, and its symbol is the delicate beauty of a frail China jar. The metamorphosis at the close, in which the lock rises above the splenetic battle and becomes an enduring source of light, is more than a wry joke. Pope has shown in small scale the ferocities that such an order can mitigate. And if it is not the stain upon honor but upon brocade that is felt like a wound, there is at least a real correspondence between those worlds of transposed scale. The players of ombre are themselves not unlike the playing-card kings and queens, and their battles and intrigues are formalized into a pattern that is more real than the actors.

The incongruity of the mock-heroic is dissolved in its even more surprising congruity, in its creation of an unheroic world of art and grace where the relative proportions are retained even as the total scale is sharply reduced. The poem does not rise to the elevation of *Windsor Forest,* for it does not seek to reconcile the least order with the highest. Instead it carries to new intensity the double vision that sees both the fragility and strength, the triviality and dignity, of art. (The elevated lock is, in a sense, the poem, shining upon beaux and sparks, but upon all others who will see it, too.) If this order remains an aesthetic one, below or beyond morality, it none the less insists upon the formal delight that is a dimension of all stable structures, whether cosmic harmonies or heroic codes, poems or patterns of civility. And it looks toward those more inclusive and morally significant visions of order that give weight to Pope's later work.

The Appeal of the Mock-Heroic: Pope and Dulness

Emrys Jones

Some of the best imaginative writing from the Restoration to about 1730 is mock-heroic or burlesque or in some way parodic in form. The mock-heroic has been very fully discussed in terms of its literary conventions, its comic use of epical situations, characters, diction, and so on, but the secret of its fascination remains not wholly accounted for. These mocking parodic forms had been available to English writers since the sixteenth century, but they have usually taken a very subsidiary place in the literary scene. But in the later seventeenth and early eighteenth centuries they seem to move to the centre of things: they attract writers of power. The result is such works as *Mac Flecknoe, A Tale of a Tub, The Battle of the Books, Gulliver's Travels,* and *The Beggar's Opera,* as well as, on a lower level, Cotton's *Virgil Travestie* and his versifications of Lucian, and such burlesque plays as Buckingham's *Rehearsal,* Gay's *What D'you Call It,* and some of Fielding's farces. Certainly no other period in English history shows such a predilection for these forms. Why were so many of the best writers of the time drawn to mock-heroic and burlesque? No doubt it is useless to look for a single comprehensive answer, but a partial explanation may be sought by considering the time, the age, itself.

The period from the Restoration to Pope's death was one whose prevailing ethos was avowedly hostile to some of the traditional uses of the poetic imagination. It disapproved of the romantic and fabulous, and saw little reason for the existence of fiction. "The rejection and contempt of fiction is rational and manly": the author is Dr. Johnson, writing in 1780,

From *Proceedings of the British Academy* 54 (1968).

but the attitude was common, even prevalent, during Pope's lifetime. The literary world into which the young Pope grew up was, it seems fair to say, relatively poor in imaginative opportunities. The poets writing immediately before Pope were without fables and without myths, except those taken in an etiolated form from classical antiquity; they seemed content with verses that made little demand on the imaginative life of their readers. It is suggestive that in his final collection of poems, *Fables Ancient and Modern* (1700), Dryden drew away from contemporary manners and affairs with versions of Ovid, Boccaccio, and Chaucer: the fabulous and romantic are readmitted through translation and imitation. Otherwise the literary scene as Pope must have viewed it as a young man was, at its best, lucidly and modestly sensible; but in feeling and imagination it was undeniably somewhat impoverished. What characterizes the literature of the Restoration is a brightly lit, somewhat dry clarity, a dogmatic simplicity; it is above everything the expression of an aggressively alert rational consciousness.

Something of this imaginative depletion can be observed in the structure of single poems. If we leave Milton aside, the poetry of the Restoration with most life in it suffers from a certain formal laxity: there is brilliance of detail but often a shambling structure. Parts are added to parts in a merely additive way, with often little concern for the whole: poems go on and on and then they stop. The poets often seem too close to actual social life, as if the poetic imagination had surrendered so much of its autonomous realm that they were reduced to a merely journalistic role; their longer poems seem to lack "inside." At one time Milton thought of Dryden as "a good rimist, but no poet." And T. S. Eliot's words still seem true of much of Dryden's verse: "Dryden's words . . . are precise, they state immensely, but their suggestiveness is often nothing."

In such a period the mock-heroic and burlesque forms seem to minister to a need for complexity. The mock-heroic, for example, gave the poet the possibility of making an "extended metaphor," a powerful instrument for poetic thought—as opposed to thought of more rationally discursive kinds. It allowed him entry into an imaginative space in which his mythopoeic faculties could be freed to get to work. And yet, while offering him a means of escape from a poetry of statement, from a superficially truthful treatment of the world around him, it at the same time seemed to guarantee his status as a sensible adult person—as a "wit"—since what arouses laughter in the mock-heroic is precisely a perception of the ludicrous incongruities between the heroic fabulous world of epic and the unheroic, nonfabulous world of contemporary society. Presumably few people nowadays think that the essence of mock-heroic is really mockery of the heroic, but neither is simply the reverse true: mockery, by means of the heroic, of the unheroic contemporary world. It would be truer to say that the mock-heroic poet—at his best, at any rate—discovers a relationship of tension between the two realms, certainly including mockery of the unheroic present, but not by any means confined to that. It might be nearer the full truth to think of him as setting out to exploit the relationship between the two realms, but ending up by calling a new realm, a new world, into being. And this new realm does not correspond either to the coherent imagined world of classical epic or to the actual world in which the poet and his readers live and which it is ostensibly the poet's intention to satirize. It is to some extent self-subsistent, intrinsically delightful, like the worlds of pastoral and romance. In various ways it gratifies an appetite, perhaps all the more satisfying for doing so without the readers' conscious awareness. And in any case, mock-heroic, with its multiple layers of integument, its inherent obliquity, was temperamentally suited to a man like Pope, who "hardly drank tea without a stratagem."

Before coming to the *Dunciad* I should like to glance at Pope's first great success in mock-heroic, *The Rape of the Lock*. It takes "fine ladies" as its main satirical subject, and the terms in which the satire works are explained in Ariel's long speech in the first canto. Since the sylphs are the airy essences of "fine ladies," Ariel's object is to impress such young ladies as Belinda with a sense of their own importance and to confirm them in their dishevelled scale of values:

> Some secret Truths from Learned Pride conceal'd,
> To Maids alone and Children are reveal'd:
> What tho' no Credit doubting Wits may give?
> The Fair and Innocent shall still believe.

Pope characteristically blurs his moral terms, so that his own position as a man of good sense is represented by the ironical phrases "Learned Pride" and "doubting Wits," whereas the empty-headed young girls have access to "secret Truths": they are "Fair and Innocent," they shall have faith. Such faith abhors any tincture of good sense, for fine ladies are characterized by an absence of good sense. They are preoccupied with their own appearance, with the outward forms of society, and—it is suggested—with *amours*. "Melting Maids" are not held in check by anything corresponding to sound moral principles; they are checked only by something as insubstantial, or as unreal, as their "Sylph." Mere female caprice or whim prevents a young girl from surrendering her honour to the importunity of rakes. Pope is working on a double standard: as readers of the poem we enjoy the fiction of the sylphs, but the satire can only work if we are also men and women of good sense who do not confuse fiction with fact—so that we do not "believe in" the sylphs any more than we "believe in" fairies. Judged from this sensible point of view, the sylphs are nothing, thin air. So in answer to Ariel's question, "What guards the purity of melting Maids?" our sensible answer is "Nothing": if a young lady rejects a man's improper proposal it is simply because—she doesn't want to accept it: she is restrained by her "Sylph." For the principles of female conduct are not rational: they are, as Ariel says, "mystic mazes," and sometimes mere giddy inconstancy will happen to keep a young lady chaste.

> When *Florio* speaks, what Virgin could withstand,
> If gentle *Damon* did not squeeze her Hand?
> With varying Vanities, from ev'ry Part,
> They shift the moving Toyshop of their Heart.

and so to the conclusive irony:

> This erring Mortals Levity may call,
> Oh blind to Truth! the *Sylphs* contrive it all.

What is the nature of Pope's poetic interest in "fine ladies" in *The Rape of the Lock*? From the standpoint of men of good sense—the "doubting Wits" of Ariel's speech—such women are silly, vain, and ignorant. They are of course badly educated: they may be able to read and write a little, but their letters, ludicrously phrased and spelt, will only move a gentleman to condescending amusement. (As Gulliver found with the Lilliputians: "Their manner of writing is very peculiar, being neither from the left to the right, like the Europeans; nor from the right to the left, like the Arabians; nor from up to down, like the Chinese; but aslant, from one corner of the paper to the other, like ladies in England.") This at least is how women, or many of them, often appeared in *The Tatler* and *The Spectator*—and how they appeared to Pope to the extent that he was a satirist. However, simply because women were less rational than men, they were also, from another point of view, more imaginative because more fanciful than their male superiors. They were more credulous, more superstitious, more given to absurd notions. For if gentlemen, or "wits," were creatures of modern enlightenment, women could be regarded as belonging to the fabulous dark ages. Accordingly what women, or women of this kind, provided for a poet like Pope, a poet working in a *mileu* of somewhat narrow and dogmatic rationalism, was a means of entry to a delightful world of folly and bad sense. For although Pope as a satirist pokes fun at them, he is yet as a poet clearly fascinated by them. Women are closer than men to the fantastic and fabulous world of older poetry, such as that of *A Midsummer Night's Dream,* and it is precisely the "fantastic" nature of women that allows Pope to create his fantastic, fairylike beings, the sylphs. *The Rape of the Lock* is full of the small objects and appurtenances of the feminine world which arouse Pope's aesthetic interest: such things as "white curtains," combs, puffs, fans, and so on. This world of the feminine sensibility is one which offers a challenge to the larger world of the masculine reason. The man of good sense might laugh at it, but he could not destroy it; and to some extent he had to recognize an alternative system of values.

The subject I have been keeping in mind is the more general one of the imaginative appeal of mock-heroic, and what I have just said about the poetic attraction of the feminine world applies also, with certain modifications, to the attraction of the *low*. The age in which Pope lived seems to have been markedly aware of the high and the low in life as in literature. The high level of polite letters, indeed the contemporary cult of politeness, and the genteel social tone of the Augustan heroic couplet seem to have coexisted with a strong awareness of what they left out below. That is to say, in this period of somewhat exaggerated politeness, correctness, rationalism, there existed a correspondingly strong interest in the low, the little, the trivial, the mean, the squalid, and the indecent—to the extent of giving all these things expression in imaginative writing. The structure of mock-heroic and burlesque forms provided a means of getting at this kind of material and thus gratifying a desire which might otherwise have been hard to reconcile with the poet's and his readers' dignity as sensible and adult men and women. For all Pope's and Swift's different intentions, one can discern something distinctly similar in Pope's sylph-attended young ladies and Swift's Lilliputians: Pope's young ladies have something of the aesthetic fascination of children's dolls, while the Lilliputians—as when the army parades on Gulliver's handkerchief—call to mind in a rather similar way the nursery world of toy soldiers; they are both enchantingly *below* our own level. *The Rape of the Lock* and Gulliver's Voyage to Lilliput are undoubtedly remarkable creative efforts: in Pope's case his poem for a good many of his readers (and not necessarily the undiscerning many) has represented the climax of his fictive powers: it has an achieved roundness, a plenitude, and an affectionate warmth, for the absence of which nothing in his later poems compensates. And yet in both works . . . the creative impulse seems close to something childish or childlike in the minds of their authors.

Belinda Ludens

William K. Wimsatt

The two stones of the Roman Neoplatonist Plotinus (*Enneads* 5.8/1.6), one beautiful in virtue of a special form carved upon it by an artist, the other endowed with being, and hence in Plotinian terms with beauty, in virtue simply of its being one thing, may be considered archetypal for a sort of metaphysical explanation which explains too much—that is to say, which expands its focus upon a special idea until that idea coincides with the whole horizon of the knowable universe. The Plotinian system has had its modern inverted counterparts in forms of expressionist idealism, notably the Crocean. I think it has another sort of parallel in the view of art, or of the whole of cultivated life, as a form of play, which develops, from the aesthetic of Kant, 1790, to a kind of climax in the masterpiece of Johann Huizinga, 1938. *Homo Ludens* asserts that "play can be very serious indeed." "Ritual," for example, "is seriousness at its highest and holiest. Can it nevertheless be play?" The trend of the argument is to say that play is the generator and the formula of all culture. It was not carrying things much further when Jacques Ehrmann, the editor of a volume in *Yale French Studies* entitled *Game, Play, Literature,* 1968, protested that Huizinga and some others were in fact taking reality too seriously. "Play is not played against a background of a fixed, stable, reality. . . . All reality is caught up in the play of the concepts which designate it." This Berkeleyan moment in the philosophy of play idealism had been in part prepared by the work of a cosmic visionary, Kostas Axelos, whose preliminaries to "planetary thinking" (*Vers la Pensée*

From *Day of the Leopards: Essays in Defense of Poems.* Yale University Press, 1976.

planetaire) of 1964 led to the simple announcement of his title page in 1969 *Le Jeu du monde*. Man as player and as toy; the universe as a game played and as itself an agent playing.

But the universe, of course, as Emerson once pointed out, is anything we wish to make it: "The world is a Dancer; it is a Rosary; it is a Torrent; it is a Boat; a Mist, a Spider's Snare; it is what you will." I myself must confess to a double inclination: to take the concept of play very broadly, yet to stop short of making it a transcendental. It seems a more useful and a more interesting concept if it has some kind of bounds and makes some kind of antithesis to something else. Surely we can think of some things, some moments of action or experience, that are not play—jumping out of the path of an ondriving truck just in time to save your life, for instance, or making out an income tax return. The more spontaneous the action, I suppose, the more certainly we can distinguish play from what is not play. Thus a sudden skip and gambol on the green is not like the leap amid the traffic. But a person filling out a tax form may conceivably, either to relieve tension or to express resentment, evolve some half-conscious overlay of irony or ritual. Allow us a moment to feel safe, and the same is true on the street. I have witnessed a very distinguished academic person—a university president—confront the rush of automobile fenders at a busy corner in New Haven by turning sidewise, like a toreador, and flaunting the skirt of his topcoat.

We have the double sense that play is both clearly different from certain other things, and that it is a chameleon—or, as Wittgenstein would put it, only a collection of family resemblances. We know that in our everyday usage *play* has not a single opposite, but a medley—what is real, serious, or necessary, what is work, war, or woe.

Perhaps we can usefully conceive the area approximately circumscribed by the term "play" as a polyhedron, in which our divisions according to genus and species will be determined by which side we think of the figure as resting on. Immanuel Kant initiated the modern discussion with a slant toward fine art when he conceived the pleasure of art as a "feeling" of freedom in the play of our cognitive faculties. Such a *play* of faculties may be analogized very widely—to the play of water in a fountain, the play of firelight on a shadowy wall, the play of muscles in an athlete's body, the play of Aristotle's taws "upon the bottom of a king of kings." The English term "play" has that loose sort of connotation. And so have the German *Spiel* and *spielen*. But the Kantian tradition of art as free play of faculties need not be frittered away in such directions. As developed by Schiller and later by Groos and Lange, it gives us a notion of manifold and ordered freedom that makes an appropriate fit for the established fine arts and at the same time may extend to such plausible analogies as childish or savage forms of mimesis, game, and ritual, and to numerous forms of civilized gratification which Kant himself snubbed as merely sensate and pleasurable or amusing.

The aesthetic or artistic emphasis on the concept of play invites us to conceive different kinds of play as realizing, with different degrees of prominence, three insistent aesthetic features: that is, expression, mimesis, and design (or pattern)—corresponding broadly to the three Kantian divisions (and features) of art: the speaking, the shaping, and the art of the beautiful play of sensation. The Kantian general aesthetic requirements of disinterest and of purposiveness without purpose reappear today in clauses concerning convention, unreality, isolation, autotelism, and freedom which make the definitions of play according to Huizinga and his successors.

"Play," however, is only one of two terms which commonly appear side by side, as if all but synonymous in recent literature of play theory. The other term is "game." The two terms are used almost interchangeably—as the French *jeu* is translated either *play* or *game*. It is my notion that the terms are not in fact synonymous, and that "play" does not always entail "game"—that "game" in fact is only one very special kind of play. Sometimes we play games; at other times, as when we gambol, or romp, or swim, or walk in the woods, or yodel, or doodle, we are just playing. At this juncture another of the inheritors of Kant and Huizinga, Roger Caillois, editor of the journal *Diogène,* comes to our aid with his articles on "play" and "games" published in 1955 and 1957. Whatever else we may say in general about play and game, however many classes or qualities of either we distinguish, two common principles seem to Caillois certain: one a childlike, spontaneous principle of improvisation and insouciant self-expression (*paidia*), the other a sort of perverse complementary principle of self-imposed obstacle or deliberate convention of hindrance (*ludus*). It is never enough, for very long, to skip and gambol. We play leapfrog or hopscotch. "The unfettered leap of joy," says Schiller, "becomes a dance; the aimless gesture, a graceful and articulate miming speech."

With convention, and only with convention, can the element of game enter into play. The idea of convention might carry us also very quickly in the direction of language, and into language games (that is to say, into the logical problem of shifting frames of reference). But a different idea from that is more relevant to my present purpose. And that is the idea of game as competition. Convention in games is the opportunity for and invitation to an orderly and limited competition.

The game of pure competitive skill (or *agōn*) and the game of chance (*alea*) are two forms of play which Caillois is specially interested in, which he would insistently distinguish, but which nevertheless he sees as very closely related. It is my own notion, though I think I need not argue it here at length, that chance has such a close affinity for competition that it is just as often an element intrinsic to some kind of competitive game (dice, poker, bridge) as it is a pure form (lottery, Russian roulette), where as Caillois instructs us, it may be conceived as inviting only the passive surrender of the player to the decree of fate.

The relation of competitive gameplay to forms of conspicuously aesthetic play may be very interesting and very difficult to state. The concept of mimesis may be the hinge on which a comparison most instructively turns. A tragic drama is a mimesis of a combat (involving often murder and war), but no combat actually occurs in this drama, at least none corresponding to that which is mimed. A game of chess or a game of bridge may be conceived as a mimic warfare (*Ludimus effigiem belli*). But that is to say that such a game proceeds according to a set of conventions which are the conditions for a very strictly limited but nevertheless *actual* combat—one which bears a relation of *analogy* to larger combats and is in that sense a *mimesis* of them. (Let nobody be in any doubt about the actuality of the combat in chess or bridge or poker.)

At least two special sorts of connection can obtain between these two sorts of play, the aesthetic and the competitive. (1) The element of combat in the sheer game can be stylized and arrested in the shape of puzzle or problem, and in this case it is altered in the direction of aesthetic design. This happens notably in the kind of compositions known as chess "problems." (2) A second kind of rapprochement is of more direct literary significance: it happens that the competitive game can appear internally to the art play, as part of the story. And here the game may be treated with either more or less precise regard for its technical details, and in either case it may manifest either more or less formal and aesthetic interest as it seems to function either more or less as an interior duplication or symbol of the gamesome or ludic nature which, in some sense, we may discover as a character of the work as a whole.

Before I plunge more directly into the proposed topic of this paper—the game of cards in Pope's *The Rape of the Lock*—let me attempt one further classical perspective, this time invoking not Plotinus but Plato himself, in an analytic mood which is pretty much the opposite of anything Neoplatonic. I have in mind that dialogue in which a rhapsode, that is, a professional declaimer of Homeric poetry and a professor of poetry, is given a destructive Socratic quizzing. The question insistently, if engagingly, pursued is this: whether a professor of poetry, or for that matter his model and inspiration the poet, knows anything at all, or has anything to teach, in his own right. It appears that he does not. If he knows anything about medicine, for instance, or about steering a ship, or spinning wool, it will be in virtue of exactly the same kind of knowledge as the practitioner of those arts would have. The mind of a poet—Homer, for instance—who talks about nearly everything, is just a grab bag of various kinds of knowledge which are the proper business of various other kinds of experts. The application is made even to the knowledge of epic games:

> "Does not Homer speak a good deal about arts, in a good many places? For instance, about chariot-driving . . . Tell me what Nestor says to his son Antilochus . . . " " 'Bend thyself in the polished car slightly to the left of them; and call to the right-hand horse and goad him on, while your hand slackens his reins.' " "Now, Ion, will a doctor or a charioteer be the better judge whether Homer speaks correctly or not in these lines?" "A charioteer, of course." "Because he has this art, or for some other reason?" "No, because it is his art."

Almost any modern reader, I suppose, is likely to believe that this question raised by Socrates is unimportant for the study of poetry. Forgetting perhaps that the Greeks of Plato's time did actually look on Homer as a chief authority about chariot racing, warfare, generalship, and related topics, and that in a sense he was such an authority, the modern reader will think of poetry about games, either outdoor or indoor games, most likely in the light of some such passage as the following near the end of the first book of Wordsworth's *Prelude,* where he recalls some of his childhood pastimes:

> Eager and never weary we pursued
> Our home amusements by the warm peat-fire
> At evening . . .
> . . . . . .
> round the naked table, snow-white deal,
> Cherry or maple, sate in close array,
> And to the combat, Lu or Whist, led on
> A thick-ribbed Army; not as in the world
> Neglected and ungratefully thrown by
> Even for the very service they had wrought,
> But husbanded through many a long campaign.

> Uncouth assemblage was it, where no few
> Had changed their functions, some, plebeian cards,
> Which Fate beyond the promise of their birth
> Had glorified, and call'd to represent
> The persons of departed Potentates.
> Oh! with what echoes on the Board they fell!
> Ironic Diamonds, Clubs, Hearts, Diamonds, Spades,
> A congregation piteously akin.
> Cheap matter did they give to boyish wit,
> Those sooty knaves, precipitated down
> With scoffs and taunts, like Vulcan out of Heaven,
> The paramount Ace, a moon in her eclipse,
> Queens, gleaming through their splendor's last decay,
> And Monarchs, surly at the wrongs sustain'd
> By royal visages.
>
> (1.534–36, 541–62)

The main thing we learn about that card game is that the cards were dog-eared, very badly beaten up—a medley of survivals from several different packs, some of them having been doctored or altered to raise their value. A poet, we will of course say, looks on a given technical routine, like playing cards, in just the light needed for whatever he is trying to say in his poem; and we will most likely imply that the precise rules and play of the game—certainly its niceties and finesses—are not likely to be a part of the poet's concern. Maybe a writer of stories about baseball—a Ring Lardner, a Bernard Malamud—will have to know what he is talking about in order to convey the appearance and feel of the thing. A very good story about chess, Vladimir Nabokov's *The Defence,* manages to create a vivid impression of a boy's experience of learning to play and of becoming a master. In Stefan Zweig's celebrated *Schachnovelle* (*The Royal Game*), the psychology of obsessive, schizoid game play seems to me less finely informed with any authentic chess experience. A story involving a card game or a chess game is likely enough to tell us something very indistinct about the game itself, or else something utterly absurd. In one story about chess that I remember, an old man is able to cheat another old man, his inveterate rival, by allowing his beard to curl about a rook at one corner of the board, thus lulling his opponent into a sense that the rook is not there. Short stories have been written indeed around the actual score of chess games—but these are just that, chess stories, and they appear for the most part in chess magazines. In one of Samuel Beckett's zero-degree novels, *Murphy,* there is the actual score of a chess game, played in a kind of madhouse, but the point of the game is its utter absurdity. Neither player (neither male nurse nor mental patient) is able to *find* the other—they play simultaneous games of solitaire. Faulkner's short story "Was" (*Go Down, Moses* [1942]) manages two hands of poker, one "Draw" and one "Stud," with an artistic economy made possible in part by the concealment and bluffing which are intrinsic to this game that gives a name to the studiously inexpressive countenance.

Wordsworth, we are told by his friend Coleridge, was a specialist in "spreading the tone." Generalization, even vagueness, in imagery, idea, and mood, was his forte. It is difficult to imagine a poem by Wordsworth in which a precise and technically correct narration of a hand at cards would have been relevant to his purpose. Is the same true for Alexander Pope? I have an idea that most of us, if only from our general habit of reading poetry, would read into Pope for the first time with no more expectation of finding an exactly described card game than in Wordsworth. I remember that when about twenty-five years ago I first studied *The Rape of the Lock* closely enough to realize fully the presence of the card game, I was very much surprised. I had a special sort of delight in the discovery—because I myself have always been moderately addicted to table games, and so it gave me pleasure to work the puzzle out—but also because the precision of the details seemed to me in a special way an achievement appropriate to Pope's art as a couplet poet and also a specially precise and exquisite miniature of this whole poem. For the modern eye or ear, this game may often pass in a somewhat sunken or muted way beneath the very colorful and rhythmic surface symbols in which the action is carried. It seems difficult to say to what degree it was hidden for Pope's readers, many of whom presumably were better up on the game of ombre than we are. For us, I think, part of the pleasure can come from the fact that the game is not awkwardly obtrusive or obviously technical, but is woven so subtly into the poetic fabric. It seems to me a merit of the passage that one may well read it without full awareness of what is going on.

There is now no way for me to avoid a degree of technicality in my exposition. The game of ombre as Pope narrates it is an impressive blend of visual technique and gamesmanship or technique according to Hoyle—the Hoyle of that day, a French book on ombre and piquet, translated into English in a volume entitled *The Court Gamester,* published at London only a few years after Pope's poem, 1719. Beginning with a writer in *Macmillan's Magazine* in 1874 and a certain Lord Aldenham, who somewhat frivolously devoted a large book to *The Game of Ombre* (3d ed., 1902), a succession of modern writers have commented on Pope's game. Geoffrey Tillotson's exposition in an appendix to his Twickenham edition of *The Rape of the Lock* in 1940 triggered a contentious correspondence in the columns of the

Times Literary Supplement. A short essay of my own, published in 1950, was an effort to tidy up the tradition and improve on it. Take a deck of cards and remove the 8s, 9s, and 10s of each suit (twelve cards in all), leaving forty. Seat three players at a table, Belinda and two male courtiers. The man to Belinda's left, probably her chief antagonist, the Baron, deals nine cards to each player (twenty-seven in all); he puts the remaining thirteen cards down in a stock or kitty. Belinda bids first, gets the bid, and declares spades trumps. The players then discard weak cards and draw an equal number of replacements from the kitty. The order of strength in the cards is not as in modern contract bridge. It differs from hand to hand, depending on which suit is trumps. For the present hand, the top card is the Ace of spades, Spadillio; next the two of spades, Manillio; next the Ace of clubs, Basto; then the spades in order, King down to three. The red aces are lower than the face cards in their suits. In order to win the hand Belinda has to take more tricks than her stronger opponent—five against four, or four against three and two.

Four tricks unroll smoothly for Belinda as she leads in succession Spadillio, Manillio, Basto, and the King of spades—pulling smaller spades from her opponents—except that on the third and fourth tricks the third player, the anonymous one, fails to come through. So the Baron may well have the last trump, the Queen. Belinda has two winning cards left in her hand, the King of hearts and the King of clubs. As the hand turns out, we can see that it doesn't matter which King she plays. She gets her fifth trick sooner or later. But what of the possibilities at that apparently crucial moment as she leads on the fifth trick? Which King shall she play?—if she is to live up to the epithet "skilful" bestowed on her by the poet at the commencement of the scene. ("The skilful Nymph reviews her Force with Care.")

We are not told every card in each player's hand. The *x*s in my chart indicate the degree of indeterminacy in Pope's specifications. But the probabilities may be considered. In the event, for instance, that the Baron has the Queen of spades and four diamonds, then no matter how the diamond tricks are divided between the Baron and the third player, producing either a win with five tricks for the Baron, or a 4–3–2 win for Belinda, or a 4–4–1 Remise or drawn game, the outcome will not *depend* upon Belinda's lead. Certain more complicated suppositions about the Baron's holding one or two low hearts or one or two low clubs (but *not* both hearts and clubs) can be made, and I have made them, I believe exhaustively. I will not recite them here. The upshot of my analysis is that only if the third player captured a diamond lead on the sixth trick and then went on to produce the 4–4–1

	BELINDA		THE BARON		SIR ANONYM
I. BELINDA →	Spadillio Ace ♠		♠		♠
II. BELINDA →	Manillio Two ♠		♠		♠
III. BELINDA →	Basto Ace ♣		♠		Plebeian Card ×
IV. BELINDA →	King ♠		Knave ♠		Pam Knave ♣
V. BARON →	King ♣		Queen ♠		×
VI. BARON →	×		King ♢		×
VII. BARON →	×		Queen ♢		×
VIII. BARON →	Queen ♡		Knave ♢		×
IX. BELINDA →	King ♡		Ace ♡		×

Remise by taking three more diamond tricks himself (the Baron throwing down low hearts or clubs—but *not* both), could Belinda suffer an *unfavorable* outcome which *depended* on her leading the wrong suit at the fifth trick. But on this supposition, that the third player held four diamonds, or perhaps on any supposition at all, Belinda at the fifth trick could suppose very little about the number of either hearts or clubs in the Baron's hand and hence would have little reason to prefer either a club or heart lead. A test by the calculus of foreseeable possibilities would be the correct test of Belinda's skill (of whether her play of the hand is, in the terms of Roger Caillois, a true *agōn* or is largely an instance of *alea*), but such a test will not quite pan out. We fall back on a more superficial, human, and plausible test by appearances. The discard of the Knave of clubs (Pam, who "mow'd down Armies in the Fights of Lu") by the third player on the fourth trick does look like a discard from weakness. Possibly his only club? In that case, the Baron may be thought somewhat more likely to have clubs than hearts. Dramatically, if not technically and mathematically, the Knave of clubs, so conspicuously heralded as a discard, advertises a certain plausibility in her next lead of the King of clubs. Belinda is a society belle and not a Charles H. Goren. It is by the standards of the polite card table (not necessarily profound) that we shall measure her skill. She is no doubt skillful in her own esteem. She leads her King of clubs, loses it to the Queen of spades. The Baron pours his diamonds apace for three tricks, his Knave on the eighth trick drawing even her Queen of hearts. Then the Baron's Ace of hearts (lower than the face cards) is forced out on the last trick, to fall a victim to the King lurking in her hand. "The Nymph exulting fills with Shouts the Sky, / The Walls, the Woods, and long Canals reply."

The pictorial features of a deck of cards, the royal faces, the plain plebeian spots, are well calculated for the symbolism of an epic battle (the "routed Army . . . / Of *Asia's* Troops, and *Africk's* Sable sons"); for that of palace revolutions ("The hoary Majesty of *Spades* . . . The Rebel-*Knave*"); and for that of the most important business of court life, the battle of the sexes (the warlike Amazonian Queen of spades, the wily Knave of diamonds, the "captive" Queen of hearts). Belinda's hubristic first sweep of four tricks, the sudden blow from fate, or the peripeteia, of the fifth trick, her narrow escape from the jaws of ruin and codille, her last-trick triumph and exultation—all these develop her portrait as the mock-heroine of a melodramatized tragic-epic action. . . .

The contrasting wider context of the big epic tradition does much of

Pope's work for him. The work is invited in a very special way by the other main part of the context, the immediate social one. It is perhaps easiest to invest literature with the colors of a game when the life represented is courtly, artificial, ritualistic, playful. Such a life, lived with a high degree of intensity and burnish, *is* a game—or a jest, as Pope and his closest friends might have said. It can also be a special sort of warfare. Pope's letter to Mrs. Arabella Fermor, prefixed to his second edition, in which the game of ombre first appears, may be read as a language game of teasing and flattery. It is not my idea that the poem itself can be said, in any useful sense, to be a game played by Pope either with himself or with his reader. The poem, however, is in a very notable way a poem about a gamesome way of life. The background life of the poem, the powders, patches, furbelows, flounces, and brocades, the smiles and curls, the china, the silver, the billet-doux, the lapdogs, and the fopperies and flirtations, are built-in elements of the higher social gamesmanship. The poem absorbs and represents this situation in a very immediate and vivid image, and thus in a very thorough sense it is a game poem.

Here we may as well recall some relevant insights of the late Dr. Eric Berne, whose best-selling book entitled *Games People Play* (1964) was developed from his less racy *Transactional Analysis in Psychotherapy* (1961). "Games" in the somewhat extrapolated but persuasive sense of certain slantwise and fictive stratagems employed in a variety of neurotic types of aggression. Instead of facing each other on the level, as adults, the role-players of Dr. Berne's analyses suffered either from assumptions of parental hauteur and inquisition or from childlike poses, sulks, and tantrums. They played, among many others, certain "Party" and "Sexual" games, to which he gave such names as "Kiss Off," "Ain't It Awful," "Rapo," "Indignation," "Let's You and Him Fight," and "Uproar." "Favors to none, to all she smiles extends."—"At every word a reputation dies."—"The Peer now spread the glittering Forfex wide."—"Then flashed the living lightning from her eyes."—"To arms, to arms! the fierce Virago cries."—"And bass and treble voices strike the skies." Let us think here also of the stubbornly contested betrothal gambits played between Congreve's Millamant and Mirabell. Think of the somberly mythologized combat between mentor and pupil, the dark luster, of Swift's *Cadenus and Vanessa*. In *The Rape of the Lock,* we witness the gladiatorial aspect of sex and courtship. Belinda "Burns to encounter two adventrous Knights, / At *Ombre* singly to decide their Doom."

The other epic games we have noticed are all highly episodic, off-center developments in the vast poems where they occur. The game of ombre occurs in a central or focal position which could be appropriate only in a poem of rococo dimensions. The game of ombre is the least deadly and most conventionalized combat in Pope's poem, and yet it is a real combat (game combats I have said and will repeat are real) and it is the most precisely delineated and most complete combat of the whole poem, appearing in the center as a kind of reducing or concentrating mirror of the larger, more important, but less decisive, kinds of strife and hints of strife that both precede and follow it.

Here perhaps we can invoke, with only a slight and forgivable degree of exaggeration, a pattern developed by Professor Cedric Whitman for ordering the complicated and lavishly repetitious procession of quarrels, councils, speeches, feasts, libations, sacrifices, battles, triumphs, defeats, and burials which make up the *Iliad* of Homer. There is a kind of center for the *Iliad* in two anomalously conjunct nighttime episodes, the embassy to Achilles of book 9 and the (perhaps genetically intrusive) reconnaissance by the scout Dolan and his violent end in book 10. Coming up to these and moving away from them are two sequences of events and of days that unfold in mirror (or butterfly) patterns of partly antithetic, partly similar images, "ring patterns." And this is in the manner of those Grecian pottery vases or urns that have friezes of figures on them converging on some central figure in a reflecting pattern (the huge vases of Dipylon ware, for instance, manufactured at about the time when Homer most likely was writing, 750 to 700 B.C.). (Or think of that "leaf-fringed legend" or "brede of marble men and maidens," priest and sacrificial heifer, that move, no doubt symmetrically from two sides, toward the "green altar" in Keats's "Ode on a Grecian Urn.")

The card game at the center of Pope's poem is not only the most precise and least earnest combat of the poem. It is at the same time, though animated, the least animate, the most completely a work of art, in that the actors described so lovingly, with such detail and color, are neither supernatural nor human agents. They are in fact only cardboard—though the ambitious animus of Belinda and the Baron are just behind them, and even the sylphs "Descend, and sit on each important Card." Move back from this artful center toward the beginning of the poem, into the second canto, and we find the human epic element of a journey or expedition (as prescribed by Bossu), Belinda's boat ride on the Thames, which is convoyed by swarms of supernatural agents, the sylphs, in attitudes of keen vigilance and readiness for combat. Look then next in the opposite direction. The game of ombre *ends* in Belinda's moment of greatest triumph. And this is followed almost immediately by the Baron's counterattack and victory as he snips off the lock. This is *his* moment of greatest triumph. (If he loses the hand at ombre, he wins the canto.) Immediately thereafter, in the fourth canto, we return to the motif of a journey, this time a descent into a grotesque allegorical region of the underworld (much as at the end of the first canto of *The Faerie Queene* of Spenser). The element of the supernatural, or preternatural, is prominent again now, both in the destination and in the traveler, who is an agent of earth, a gnome, descending to the Cave of Spleen on no benevolent mission.

Now move back to the very beginning of the poem, the first canto. After the opening epic invocation, we first get our bearings in a scene of the human and comic everyday, with Belinda and her dog, rousing at noon to an afternoon of adventure. In the first canto, too, appear the epic elements of extended discourse and encyclopedic knowledge, and of supernatural agency, as the doctrine concerning the elemental spirits is expounded by the guardian sylph, with premonitions of impending disaster. At the end of the canto, Belinda with the assistance of Betty arms herself like an epic hero for battle and at the same time practices her ritual of self-worship at the toilet table. At the level of such motifs, perhaps we must admit that a degree of sinuosity complicates our pursuit of an overall symmetry. The chief later moments of ritual, for instance, occur in the second canto with the Baron's piled up French romances, the gloves and garters sacrificed to the power of Love, and in the ombre canto with the ceremony of the coffee mill and "altars of Japan." We have what may perhaps be called only a complementary pattern of different emphasis, when we observe that the extended anaphoristic sequences of hyperbole and bathos ("While Fish in Streams, or Birds delight in Air, / Or in a Coach and Six the *British* Fair"), both in the author's own voice and in the voices of Belinda, the Baron, Thalestris, and Clarissa, are a conspicuous feature of the second half of the poem, beginning at the end of the third canto and recurring through the fourth and at the start of the fifth. But with these sustained speeches, especailly with the inflammatory speech of Thalestris to Belinda near the end of the fourth canto and the ensuing episode of the vacuous Sir Plume's confrontation with the Baron, we are on lowly human and comic ground again, in a position roughly the counterpart of the opening of the poem in our geometric scheme. (The speeches as such may be set against the long initial discourse of the sylph.) The comic vein is conspicuously continued in the fifth and last canto with the lecture on good humour delivered by Clarissa and rejected by Belinda, and in the closing furious pitched battle between the belles and beaus.

The fury of this combat has no counterpart in the first half of the poem.

We may say that the airy hints of danger and the vigilance in the first two cantos have been stepped up by the gamesome duel of the third canto, to a degree of violence where the Baron's rude aggression and the ensuing turmoil are poetically plausible. And now Pope finds himself in a special dilemma, and with also a special opportunity for brilliance, in this noisy combat. The more physically it is realized, the less it can be satisfactorily resolved. And so, as shouts "To Arms," clapping fans, rustling silks, and cracking whalebones shade into death at the eyes of fair ones, a show of Homeric gods in epic simile, and an allusion to Jove's "golden Scales in Air," weighing the "Men's Wits against the Lady's Hair," the strife shifts into the mode of metaphor and symbol, or of myth—like so many irresolvable combats we have known in story and on stage. Belinda resorts to throwing a physical pinch of snuff at the Baron and even threatens him with a deadly bodkin. But the only injury inflicted is a huge sneeze, which reechoes to the high dome. Apparently on the waves of sound or air generated by this sneeze, or by Belinda's cry of "*Restore the Lock,*" which too rebounds from the vaulted roofs, the Lock itself mounts and disappears. "But trust the Muse—she saw it upward rise, / Tho' mark'd by none but quick Poetic Eyes." Like a "sudden Star," or a comet, it "shot thro' liquid Air, / And drew behind a radiant *Trail of Hair.*" Vanished, it assumes the mythic proportions of the founder of Rome, Romulus, who withdrew to the heavens during a thunderstorm, or the constellated locks of the Egyptian queen Berenice (virtuously sacrificed for the safety of her husband), or the planet Venus worshiped by lovers at the Lake in St. James's Park.

Variation in kinds of combat is one of the main structural modes, or principles of progression, in this poem. The minutely delineated cardboard combat of the central canto is the concave mirror in which, as Samuel Johnson might have put it, the ultimately sidereal reaches of the rest of the poem (the sun of the first three cantos, the stars of the last) are focused—and clarified. Or, to shift my metaphor, and to bring in the concluding words of the short essay which I wrote on the poem twenty years ago: "The game of Ombre expands and reverberates delicately in the whole poem. The episode is a microcosm of the whole poem, a brilliant epitome of the combat between the sexes which is the theme of the whole."

Uniting Airy Substance: *The Rape of the Lock* 1712–1736

Robin Grove

The critical engines have not proved fatal yet: Pope is a great deal more agile than his commentators. But then, he knew he needed to be so. He took their measure early, issuing them with Discourses on Pastoral, "Keys" to his works, or parodies of their own apparatus. ("The *Machinery*, Madam, is a Term invented by the Criticks.") Yet despite his efforts the Aristarchs marched on until he must have wondered if any power could stop them, the triumph of the mighty academic Dunces seeming to ensure all poets are to be laid low:

> Turn what they will to Verse, their toil is vain,
> Critics like me shall make it Prose again
> (*Dunciad*, 4.213–14)

—except that Bentley's proud threat in its moment of utterance is turned *back* into wit, by Pope.

It is this wit, able to catch and transform pedantry itself, which makes one hope critics need not abdicate entirely, uncomfortable though we must feel under such a writer's eye. Instead we might take our cue from the criticism Pope practised on his own productions. For there we have the chance to grasp, not in theory but in living practice, the nature of his creative enterprise. It is something more fallible than he may have thought. In fact his verse turns out to be surprisingly uneven, once the high finish of its couplets has ceased to dazzle us. On the other hand, Pope's habit of "revising

From *The Art of Alexander Pope*, edited by Howard Ershine-Hill and Anne Smith.

and re-vising," as F. W. Bateson has called it, is evidence not so much of failure narrowly avoided ("an erratic stylistic sense") as of the unusual closeness of the critic in him to the creative writer. Much the most interesting revisions are those where creativity, as we watch, renews itself by repossessing and reshaping what it has already made. To call this activity "criticism" hardly seems generous enough; yet that is what it is; and it is so impressive in Pope that, far from his being overrated now, he seems almost unrecognized as the extraordinarily flexible poet-critic he is.

Nowhere more active than in *The Rape of the Lock,* which not only provides, like *The Dunciad,* shorter and longer versions for comparison but, being his first sustainedly great work, shows his genius seized by the opportunity growing in confidence and power. In humanity too, and self-understanding. So the methodizing orator of the *Essay on Criticism* gives place to a poet whose good nature, as well as his moral sense, appears in what he made of the commission to laugh two families together again. What may have begun as a jeu d'esprit to be tossed aside once their breach was healed, assumed unexpected significance under his hand. Already he had transformed the quarrel itself; now, over the next years, he transformed the poem too, extending, revising, omitting—turning whatever was left of original pain into greater beauty and laughter.

Thus its history is as follows. The poem was probably begun during August 1711, and the author later said it took him less than a fortnight to compose. But no publication occurred until May 20, 1712, and Pope's rueful complaint (it "has been so long coming out, that the Ladies Charms might have been half decay'd, while the Poet was celebrating them, and the Printer publishing them") suggests he could revise at leisure what he had composed in such dextrous haste. Whether or not he did rework the poem at this point however he was certainly rethinking it soon after it appeared. His burlesque *Receit to make an Epick Poem,* in the *Guardian* of June 10, 1713, is one clue to that, and by December 8 of the same year he is writing to Swift that the revisions to the *Lock* are complete. This second version, in five cantos not two, was released in March 1714, and within four days had sold "to the number of three thousand, and is already reprinted." A third edition—in effect, another reprinting—followed in July; a fourth which did introduce minor changes, mainly of punctuation, came just over a year later, in September 1715, by which date Pope was claiming sales in excess of six thousand copies. Public interest in the poem clearly kept pace with the author's own. The last substantial revision to it was made for his collected *Works,* 1717, an edition which not only intensified the effect of earlier rewritings but added Clarissa's thirty lines in canto 5, "to open more clearly the MORAL of the Poem." With that, Pope's revisions were virtually complete. His few later emendations, with one exception perhaps, promote ease rather than increased richness of reading. We are left therefore with three significant texts: *The Rape of the Locke* (hereafter *Locke,* or 1712); the version of 1714 which introduces the Sylphs; and (1717) the poem more or less as we have it today. The overlappings and metamorphoses show us Pope's imagination reimagining a piece already so finished that, in one critics's judgment, he could not hope to better it, and so should leave well alone.

I

Addison's advice, though it irritated Pope, was obviously sincere. The *Locke* is a beautifully accomplished poem which makes so much of its slight material that no one would predict its author could make more. And as it happens, a modern reader taking up the standard text might scan its first dozen lines without realizing how new a poem this version, post-1717, is. But whereas lines 13–14 originally read:

> *Sol* thro' white Curtains did his Beams display,
> And op'd those Eyes which brighter shine than they
> (1712)

—and that was how things stayed in 1714—now, in the latest version of the poem, a different action is commenced:

> *Sol* thro' white curtains shot a tim'rous ray,
> And op'd those eyes that must eclipse the day.
> (1717)

The changes are not extensive. Both couplets gallantly flatter Belinda, and the first has if anything a more forthright energy. But only in the later version does the Sun himself offer the masculine compliment of "shooting" his Ray through her Curtains, to turn tentative as he touches them and gently enters in. He has *cause* to be timorous this time, when her eyes eclipse Nature's own light: day itself—with which we reach astronomical grandeurs hardly realized in the sunrise of version 1. Trope here, in 1717, approaches Metaphysical conceit; but Pope's decorum creates something unlike any earlier good morrow. For the outside universe, like the sexual awareness of writer and reader, graciously keeps its place: sunlight trembles to enter Belinda's room; its fierceness hesitates, then quietens, crossing the line-break to "ope" her eyes so gravely; and Pope's amusement tenderly encompasses it all. He has, rewriting, strengthened both the ardour of the sun and the power of Belinda's beauty, while the harmonic consciousness of the Augustan couplet, composing things into so luminous a whole, enables him to distribute through the phrasing more mockery and more praise both at once. Nor does he choose between them. Rather, delight and irony intensify each other, and the couplet form itself shines brighter in his mind the more daring the range of innuendo it contains.

So it will be my argument that what opened before Pope as he strove with his poem was a new sense of the aesthetic (which in this case is to say, the human) issues entailed in his mock-heroic world. In fact, mock-heroic itself, the superior irony it implies, is questioned and explored: as in the present couplet. For the Belinda of 1712 is the possessor of eyes so conventionally marvelous that they are, merely, "brighter" than the sun. It took Pope some time to see that simple increase or diminution, the trick of mock-heroic, would never be enough. The ironies it yields are telling, but too easy. Hence the quite different order of metaphoric play in the revision of 1717, where in place of quantification comes active, sexual beauty—Belinda's of course, but surely the sungod's as well: each inviting the other's advance, although to accept would be to be mastered or eclipsed. At one stroke now, the ambiguous drama of the poem is ready to waken into life, leaving mock-heroic for the sake of pleasures of a subtler, more poignant kind. To achieve that certainly took more than local smoothing of the verse. Nor do we appreciate the revisions if we stress only Pope's large reforms, such as the insertion of the Sylphs, and the card game, and Clarissa's "good Humour" speech. Pope was proud of his new Machinery, as Warburton reports, but pleased most of all that he had prepared the poem to receive it and was able to make it work. So his first rewritings prepare us also to receive his imagination's most audacious creatures.

No doubt it's for this reason that he worked so minutely over the opening sequences themselves.

> What dire Offence from Am'rous Causes springs,
> What mighty Quarrels rise from Trivial Things,
> I sing—This Verse to *C—l,* Muse! is due;
> This, ev'n *Belinda* may vouchsafe to view:
> Slight is the Subject, but not so the Praise,
> If she inspire, and He approve my Lays.
>
> (1.1–6; 1712)

Read one way, the lines have truly epic sonority and syntax; for a moment they bring what the age had been taught to recognize as Homeric passions into sight. Next moment, though, the mighty subject just proposed is mocked, its "dire" threat emerging from trivial things and offset by the twangling music of a modern bard endeavouring to pluck impressive noises from an instrument inadequate to the task (*springs / Things / sing*). It makes such a good joke that the author is willing to bear the cacophony. ("Amrus cauzis . . . Horrible!" Tennyson wailed, "I would sooner die than write such a line.") But while critics as fine-eared as he and Bateson regret the dissonance, Pope more wittily retains it through all his emendations—if only because a reader accustomed to Grand Style needs to be kept on guard. Otherwise, he will din himself into accepting anything, even the next couplet, so long as it's pitched high enough.

> Slight is the Subject, but not so the Praise,
> If she inspire, and He approve my Lays.

A compliment certainly to Belinda and Caryll: between them they make whatever a poet does worthwhile; but this gallantry contains an insolence that dares them to notice it—so slight a subject for the verse as she is, and he so undiscriminating that he'll approve effusions regardless of merit or fault. If a final compliment survives, it does so by winning its way through audacities like this.

In all, it would be wrong to call this first opening to the poem less than brilliant. The only doubt might be as to its equilibrium: whether the manner isn't too heavily loaded against the matter, the shuttling from Epic to Commonplace too briskly demeaning? So it is interesting to gather Pope's own sense of justice hadn't been satisfied either. In 1714 he removes some of the heavy emphasis compelled on the reader by over-frequent capitals. 1717 brings a more inward-reaching change; for now the poem opens not with "Quarrels"—"What mighty Quarrels rise from Trivial Things" (1.2; 1712)—but with a more questioning line: "What mighty contests rise from trivial things" (1717). The alteration is slight: one word; but where the original had the ring of contempt about it (merely, what happened between the Petre and Fermor families), the later noun is hoveringly suggestive: more resonant, because more abstract. For "Contest" takes many shapes, from heroic *agon* to petty squabble, and the new word leaves the ironies open, where the earlier had witheringly closed them off.

Couplet by couplet, then, Pope strives beyond his "history" into the larger significance that history contained. And as the poem increases in power, so do we as readers, its demands extending our capacities too, until in the quarrels over Arabella Fermor's hair we glimpse those graver conflicts in which virginity indeed is rent, and, simultaneously, fulfilled. Of course such innuendo was always present; the phrasing is *very* explicit, from the title, daring the reader to take it seriously, down to the "softest bosoms" and the play on Belle Fermor's name:

> Say what strange Motive, Goddess! cou'd compel
> A well-bred *Lord* t'assault a gentle *Belle*?
> (1.7–8; 1712)

The poet's problem is to keep the implications of his language active but at bay—and in this the knowingness of mock-heroic was a positive liability, edging couplets towards the very cynicism decorum would suppress. Pope took years arriving at any solution. Even now, his apostrophe to the Goddess is one point where the poem slightly grates. Yet the irony he finally achieved turns mock-heroic back against itself, which was what he needed to do. For what produced indecorousness in the first place was this inflated style's refusal to be kept down: it *will* call the spoiling of a hairstyle an "assault," a "rape," and the only way for 1712 to dismiss the shadow of reality thus roused was to make the actors seem incapable of sexual feats of the kind. Hence the sarcastic reduction:

> And dwells such Rage in *softest Bosoms* then?
> And lodge such daring Souls in *Little Men*?
> (1.11–12; 1712)

Warton and others say Pope refers to short Lord Petre here; and certainly mock-heroic is keen to measure discrepancies, setting mighty Souls against their lack of inches. So this particular sneer survives in all the editions looked at so far. Not till 1736 when the last telling change to the canto was made does Pope escape the superior "heartless" manner mock-heroic had imposed. He does escape however, by taking on himself the force of the jibe directed, till then, *away* from the clever poet. Now, that critical sense which is morality-in-practice involves him also in the irony, and syntax is reworked to include not just Belinda, the Baron, and the poetic Muse, but the poet's own vulnerable self. Just for a moment the verse admits that "lively little creature, with long Arms and Legs: a Spider is no ill emblem of him": the tiny poet "*Dick Distick* by Name" whose caricature Pope had drawn in *The Guardian* No. 92, and the self-image of the homunculus, painful and absurd, is gathered into the suavity of the lines. A quarter of a century after they were first laid down, the couplets are made to run as follows (and a footnote inserted to draw attention to the change):

> Say what strange motive, Goddess! could compel
> A well-bred Lord t'assault a gentle *Belle*?
> Oh say what stranger cause, yet unexplor'd,
> Cou'd make a gentle *Belle* reject a Lord?
> In tasks so bold, can little men engage,
> And in soft bosoms dwells such mighty Rage?
>
> (1736)

The "tasks" include those laid on the poet himself, whose most adventurous powers are needed if he is, thus engaged, to proclaim what the Goddess will reveal. Pope too becomes one of the little men who rise to bold undertakings, but on his own creative terms.

II

The revisions one on another of these opening lines show a poet fighting free of mock-heroic in order to establish the manner *appropriate* for an incident which, realistically viewed, makes any concern about it seem absurd. "Slight is the subject," Pope admits. But then, realism itself is one of the attitudes the poem calls in question. It always did. Even the original *Locke* mocks naturalism with great *brio*; the trouble is, it still retains a quasi-naturalistic form. Thus the ordinary world is not so much transformed as derided by the "epic" beauties superimposed on it. And the discrepancy between the two is pointed up by the brisk transitions propelling the story forward.

> *Sol* thro' white Curtains did his Beams display,
> And op'd those Eyes which brighter shine than they;
> *Shock* just had giv'n himself the rowzing Shake,
> And Nymphs prepar'd their *Chocolate* to take;
> Thrice the wrought Slipper knock'd against the Ground,
> And striking Watches the tenth Hour resound.
> *Belinda* rose, and 'midst attending Dames
> Launch'd on the Bosom of the silver *Thames*.
>
> (1.13–20; 1712)

Sunrise to embarkation takes only three couplets. Pope's instinct was right when he postponed the voyage, transferring it to what became canto 2. But even with this prolongation of poetic time the new poem 1714, fails to make the most of the world he is venturing upon. Like 1712, it spends its skill edging the narrative forward, happy with the neat *appearance* of making points.

> *Sol* thro' white Curtains did his Beams display,
> And op'd those Eyes which brighter shine than they;
> Now *Shock* had giv'n himself the rowzing Shake,
> And Nymphs prepar'd their *Chocolate* to take;
> Thrice the wrought Slipper knock'd against the Ground,
> And striking Watches the tenth Hour resound.
> *Belinda* still her downy Pillow prest,
> Her Guardian *Sylph* prolong'd the balmy Rest.
> (1.13–20; 1714)

As yet, nothing much is generated by the bringing together of Belinda and Sol, Nymphs and lapdog. If anything, a smoother rhythm—"Now *Shock* . . . "—weakens the briskness with which the little creature first started into life. And for most of the passage the halves of each couplet adhere in demure ironies with nowhere significant to go. Pope is too concerned with getting his new actors, Ariel and the others, onto stage to be fully alert to the beauty and ridiculousness of the world awakening inside his verse. Only when his expansion of the poem was complete, and Belinda and the Sylphs secure, did his imagination, reinspired by them, return to play over opportunities missed before. Not till 1717 do the Nymphs disappear (called to a far better joke at their entry in canto 1, l. 62) and little dog Shock become one of a *class* of pampered creatures, all knowing what fashion demands of them and ready to meet its ordinances on the stroke of the clock. It is a breathtaking metamorphosis.

> *Sol* thro' white curtains shot a tim'rous ray,
> And op'd those eyes that must eclipse the day;
> Now lagdogs give themselves the rowsing shake,
> And sleepless lovers, just at twelve, awake:
> Thrice rung the bell, the slipper knock'd the ground,
> And the press'd watch return'd a silver sound.
> (1.13–18; 1717)

The watches of earlier versions simply told the time. Now, their very mechanism's delicacy is felt, returning its "silver" sound to the finger's pressure. All sensuous response is heightened, to make the beauties of the passage tender, intense and ample in quite new ways. Here the sungod himself parts curtains and eyelids timorously, only to deepen the luxury of balmy rest. No longer hurried through the jokes, we are allowed to catch lovers and lapdogs waking absurdly on time, yet to feel also the innocence of Belinda's sleep, untouched in its perfection, shaded by pure curtains, and not quite broken as the faint chimes measure the end of her virginal repose. Even as the world around her stirs, the one soft pressure, to awake, is reciprocated by the pressure of her dream and her head on its downy pillow. And this moment suspended between worlds makes way for the entry of her Sylph. "Thrice rung the bell, the slipper knock'd the ground"—those fragile dotted-rhythms are an overture to the airy substance, the thin glittering textures of the sylphic vision.

Pope's changes in short ensure that the Sylphs are introduced to a poem, a reader, prepared for the miraculous to happen. Already, before Ariel appears, the sights and sounds of normality are being transfigured, which was necessary if the poem were to move beyond mock-epic. For inherent in the structure of a world "naturalistically" portrayed are assumptions which make any quarrel over a lock of hair look ridiculously small. Whereas what Pope came to see in his poem as he remade it over and over again was something beyond a jest. Even naturalism with its disturbing appetites and touching inadequacies is left behind as satire opens into ambiguous celebration.

To be sure, the Belinda of 1712 had been captivating ("Love in these Labyrinths his Slaves detains"), but she was something of a pantomime virago too. By contrast, the Belinda of 1714 is exquisite, pitiable, and threatened. Yet so long as the poem remained story-bound the realisms of time and place, discrepancies between inflated statement and all-too-trivial deed, were liable to reemerge and dispatch her. Therefore Pope creates a world whose *every* aspect is transformed. Inside Belinda's bedroom (itself raised to new beauty) he evokes her sleep, and within the interior time of that, her dream. The Sylphs who now enter the poem exist in their own element, hardly subject to mortal pains.

III

From here on Pope's revisions are less a matter of rewriting lines and couplets than of his bringing into the poem such unforeseen vivacities that its proportions are quite changed. Almost nothing of 1712 is actually discarded, so we see the more clearly the effect of its new environment, where the carried-over poetry feels so very different. What has happened is a shift in gravity, so to speak. Its centre is placed, not in mock-epic, but in Sylphs (of all creatures) who do their utmost to control events even as events take Belinda away from them, into the social world. Of course, seen from one angle Society is the very arena in which the Sylphs desire her to shine: on their terms only, though. Thus, as she wakes from her morning dream, to pass to the dressing table, thence to the barge and card party, rape and final battle—five stages of progressive engagement in the dangerous world of the sexes—so her progress is mapped out yet at the same time shielded by five insertions of sylphic matter, one to each new canto. But the importance of these diminishes as the poem goes on. Occupying most of the foreground in canto 1, the Sylphs are little by little displaced until, in canto 5, they attract only a glance or two before the battle ends. So we watch them give way to cards, lovers, spleen and even speeches. Yet even so, the extent of their jurisdiction isn't easily defined. Maybe they *are* limited to standing by, as Dr. Johnson thought: powerless to affect action in any way that counts. On the other hand, their power over the vanity of the human heart increases as events go on. And as for the poem's climax, if the Lock must be lost (as it must) its translation to the sky beyond the reach of any Ravisher is just the compromise which would please them most. For although the Sylphs withdraw in the closing sequences, neither the Lords *nor* the Ladies who are left have won.

Such equivocation is typical. Even Pope's original *Locke* makes "realism" about the fops and belles of modern society no very simple thing. Measured against Homeric heroes, these contemporaries of ours appear preposterously small: we must be realistic about them. But then, doesn't the light of common day show up past grandeur too, making us wonder if we are realistic about *it*? For whatever anyone did at great Anna's Hampton Court, some divinity or hero in Homer, Virgil, Milton, had done it before—a comparison which necessarily works both ways. So far, so complex. In 1714 these ironies redouble. They endure no breach but an expansion, into something more luminous and airy still. For the new poem sets a parallel below the human scale, as well as one above. We move not just among divinities now, but sylphids who, so much smaller, more delicate than humanity, provide their own commentary on it, and on its Homeric counterparts. The "humbler province" of these spirits is to tend the Fair, waging campaigns, not to avenge an epic wrong but to protect brocade. At the same time, though, we should not underestimate these battles. Just because of their tiny size they hold a kind of terror, as sylphic consciousness receives the brunt of happenings which to human sight hardly signify at all. "To save the Powder from too rude a Gale" takes courage if the lightest zephyr *is* a gale, not in poetic hyperbole (our gross point of view), but as experienced by translucent fluttering Sylphs. And so with the most delicately miniature events. The intensity with which delight, pain, danger, are felt by these filmy bodies makes the Sylphs' world momentarily vast, like wilds *inside* the "crystal" of the air.

> Some in the fields of purest *Aether* play,
> And bask and whiten in the Blaze of Day.
> (2.79–80; 1714)

An exquisite vulnerability (the condition of the creatures' freedom) is registered as they "whiten" in the Blaze of Day, sensitive even to the point of extinction.

To call such beings the "Machinery" of the poem is engagingly sly, but Pope's witticism reminds us how fine and multiple are the ways by which he mingled their insubstantial presence into the human drama. Had we not had the *Locke* of 1712 for comparison, we might never have been alerted to the Sylphs' seductions of tempo itself. But as against the briskness with which the heroine was first sent on her way the moment the clocks struck ten—

> *Belinda* rose, and 'midst attending Dames
> Launch'd on the Bosom of the silver *Thames*
> (1.19–20; 1712)

—the revised poem allows her morning rituals all the time in the world. In fact sylphic episodes in general are marked by suspension or tremulous pause. It is when the necessities of bodily life are allayed—when people do not *have* to wake, or get themselves somewhere, or eat from sheer hunger—that the Sylphs' opportunity appears. In spite of which it is above all these fastidious spirits who manifest the body's power. To them, all physicality may be threatening, but not even fine-dressed fops and ladies concern themselves more with the preciousness of bodily life. With the Sylphs' arrival in 1714 Belinda's living beauty is realized to the full as, surrounded by them at her dressing table, laying artifice upon artifice, she grows lovelier while we watch. Nor is that loveliness mere daubing, as Dennis protested in his bad tempered *Remarks on Mr. Pope's Rape of the Lock,* 1728. Belinda assisted by these Celestials in painting a "purer" blush on her cheeks is practising no fraud on nature, but bringing forth what nature is capable of, in an ideal world.

> Repairs her Smiles, awakens ev'ry Grace,
> And calls forth all the Wonders of her Face.
> (1.141–42; 1714)

Unaided realism could not see those wonders though, or make us respect her, if it were not for the Sylphs. In canto 1 we have just begun to feel their presence, hardly accustomed as yet to the diminutive intensities of experience as proved on sylphic pulses. Tactfully, Pope reserves some of his best jokes in that style for episodes still to come. Yet already he is preparing us to realize what the world to Sylph-consciousness might be like.

> This Casket *India's* glowing Gems unlocks,
> And all *Arabia* breaths from yonder Box.
> The Tortoise here and Elephant unite,
> Transform'd to *Combs,* the speckled and the white.
> Here Files of Pins extend their shining Rows,
> Puffs, Powders, Patches, Bibles, Billet-doux.
> (1.133–38; 1714)

Two perspectives are present here. By one, the world's spaciousness is ludicrously reduced: continents only aids to vanity; Arabia itself distilled to a perfume, and even that put away in a box. From another angle, though, closer to the "essence" of things, the dressing table is a wonder of sensuous life. What fragrance is released by that tender verb, "And all *Arabia* breaths"; the very pins allure the eye, drawing up in miniature formation to "extend their shining Rows"; while as for the purpose behind the boudoir's array, the verse is alert to the merest hint—as when it catches Tortoise and Elephant coupled in love-play, before the prudent explanation ("*Combs*") returns the stage to rights. We may not be ready to view the scene as Sylphs do, but the episode foreshadows something of what such visions might be like.

Yet even so, our delight in the Sylphs and what they make of feminine beauty is carefully restrained. Pope is aware of Belinda with an admiration fuller, more delicate than theirs, though it permits him to be critical with a gravity her aerial flatterers never approach at all.

> And now, unveil'd, the *Toilet* stands display'd,
> Each Silver Vase in mystic Order laid.
> First, rob'd in White, the Nymph intent adores
> With Head uncover'd the *Cosmetic* Pow'rs.
> A heav'nly Image in the Glass appears,
> To that she bends, to that her Eyes she rears.
> (1.121–26: 1714)

The Sylphs encourage this strange separation of self from appearance, and to their blandishments Belinda is only too ready to succumb. Succumb she does, moreover; but not entirely. For Pope genuinely does allow her freedom. Compared to the verse the Sylphs attract, the ampler quieter movements of the writing here open a silence around Belinda, even amid her self-regard. The emphasis falls less on the vanity of her devotions than on the slow ritual movements by which living figure and mirror-image answer one another. Her reflection itself "appears" as if of its own volition, and there is a self-forgetfulness in the posture of the girl, rapt before this beautiful Other who is distanced as well as disclosed by her glass. In all, she is touchingly innocent, as though fashionable Society really were a *pastorale* where fine ladies appear as Nymphs, not in spite of their cosmetic arts but because of them indeed.

All the same, as this triumph of modishness shows, there is a dismaying side to the obligatory "innocence" of a belle. She must attract men—to be irresistible is her *raison d'être;* and yet no whisper of notoriety must blow on her, since reputation is a tissue so fine it is easily spoilt forever, and Appearances (if nothing else) must be kept intact. Even should she "yield" to a lover, therefore, that must be made a victory too. The successful beauty never gives herself away. So we begin to see the perilous balance a Belinda must maintain. The perfection of her virginity is something to be treasured. Whether as the Sylphs would cherish and adorn it, though, is another matter. For they teach armed frigidity.

> Favours to none, to all she Smiles extends,
> Oft she rejects, but never once offends.
> Bright as the Sun, her Eyes the Gazers strike,
> And, like the sun, they shine on all alike.
> (2.11–14; 1714)

Brilliance and poise are what the Sylphs admire: a femininity able to excite but endlessly refuse; and its quality is well suggested by that hard verb, "strike." At this point however it needs to be said that precisely this was the nature of Belinda's triumph in the first, presylphic poem too. In 1712, 1.27–30, her dazzling appearance on the barge occurs in just these terms—a fact which helps us grasp what happened to material Pope carried over from earlier to later version.

It is rather like the situation described in Eliot's famous essay.

> The existing order is complete before the new work arrives; for order to persist after the supervention of novelty, the *whole* existing order must be, if ever so slightly, altered.

When Pope revised the *Locke* of 1712, something new was made not only in rewritten or added verse, but also out of poetry left untouched. That is, the changed context changed our reading even of lines which remained the same. And indeed Pope's own sense of what he'd created in 1712 altered as his understanding of Belinda grew. She had always been accorded a suitably double-edged praise; he now say how much *more* troubling those ironies became, once drawn into the orbit of the Sylphs. Who better than they to applaud the frigidity of the coquette, armed for conquest and victorious in her disdain of every suitor? On the other hand, who better than Sylphs to reflect the transience of beauty, touchingly ephemeral no matter how exploited or misused? In a poem alive with such creatures, Belinda's own beauty is refracted and heightened again by "thousand bright Inhabitants of Air." We have not exactly left the world of Fashion and current cliché; rather, we are enabled to *see* its hyperboles, and feel the implications of their sensuous force, as if for the first time. So it is with the compliment to Belinda's dazzling eyes. In the poem of 1712 such praise was *de rigueur:* "lively Looks," radiant noncommittal smiles, all part of the conventional armoury of the belle. By 1714 however the ironies of that language are persuaded into the narrative drama itself. Compliment and metaphor are so far mythologized that they become presences in their own right, imaginary landscapes (almost) which Sylphs at least might inhabit. Thus the Thames voyage in the newly conceived canto 2 opens with a passage of operatic splendour.

> Not with more Glories, in th'Etherial Plain,
> The Sun first rises o'er the purpled Main,
> Than issuing forth, the Rival of his Beams
> Lanch'd on the Bosom of the Silver *Thames.*
>
> (2.1–4; 1714)

Restoration gallantry, with its "Goddesses" and "Nymphs," now finds itself put to the test. Belinda, to eyes adjusting themselves to sylphic vision, seems "divine" indeed. Of course, the poetry is careful to suggest what is dubious about such glories: the florid Drydenesque of the lines is, by Pope's own standards, in poor taste, the Sylphs being conservative-vulgar in literary matters as in others, I suspect. Yet what living metaphors are released. Through the eulogy, Homeric amplitude is gained by common day ("th'Etherial Plain"), while Belinda, seen to be heavenly as is a belle's prerogative, gives light to all the world, even her satellites ("Fair Nymphs, and well-drest Youths around her shone") gleaming not with the light of their own finery, as they did in 1712, but with that of *her* beams, received and given back to add to her proper glory. It is as though the very tropes acclimatize themselves to a poem containing Sylphs and, in doing so, reveal intensities we never knew they held.

No such coherence governs action in the poem of 1712. There, Belinda rises, embarks, and after the (inset) Baron's sacrifice, her arrival at Hampton Court is simply announced: "Close by those Meads for ever crown'd with Flow'rs" (1.65; 1712). Tempo is a matter of moving the story forward. Whereas by 1714 each "soft transition" helps to create new meaning. Hidden metaphors are released; the Baron performs his sacrifice to Love, and this time the object of his prayers comes in view: a moment of pause not thought of when Belinda made her original journey.

> But now secure the painted Vessel glides,
> The Sun-beams trembling on the floating Tydes,
> While melting Musick steals upon the Sky,
> And soften'd Sounds along the Waters die.
> Smooth flow the Waves, the Zephyrs gently play [,]
> *Belinda* smil'd, and all the World was gay.
>
> (2.47–54; 1714)

Floating, poised, the "painted Vessel" is as much Belinda as the barge she rides in, and we feel the precarious balance of them both as, "secure" on trembling sunbeams, they bear their precious freight. Nothing more beautifully embodies the values upheld by so much Augustan art: the smoothness of surface, the "social" aplomb, the yielding sentiment exquisitely restrained by decorum. We might almost call Belinda herself, like the poetry in which she is created, a Metaphor for the politeness of high eighteenth-century civilization.

But that *is* too abstract. Pope's verse is content to assemble a fine variety of poetical Device, all the way from Heroic to lyrical-popular, and then at the proper moment divert attention from itself, in honour of Belinda. Neither the poetry nor she need be treated as "metaphor" for anything else, since they are both so alive themselves. With Belinda, however, the question remains, what will she make of that life? For seemingly she holds herself aloof. "Favours to none, to all she Smiles extends": that is the Goddess who is carrried on the barge, indifferently smiling on all alike. Being a Goddess, the imperturbable ease which Fashion decrees and well-bred Literature seeks is already hers, and it protects her from any discomforting approach. Yet the verse throbs on every side with contrary undermeanings: "trembling," "melting," "soften'd"—the language of sentimental romance, climaxing in its favoured euphemism, "die." The Belinda who outwardly is all uncommitted elegance now seems, should her weakness be discovered, only too ready to succumb; an estimate which again applies to the Augustan art the lines ironically represent (the chiasmus of 1.51, "Smooth flow the

Waves" is noticeably elegant-sentimental). With either party, however, Pope is too polite to insist. He provides something more fascinating than mockery: a transition to the region of the Sylphs through, of all things, the clichés which betray the belle's secret romantic heart.

We might have supposed the Sylphs would have nothing to do with worldly amours. "Reject Mankind" is after all the doctrine they have preached. But what leads to *sylphic* chastity, it turns out, is the very language of flirtation, "playing" on the scene to heighten it as no other hyperbole could. Meltingly tender attitudes are struck; sunbeams tremble, senses interchange till music steals upon the Sky and sound expires in Water. And these ardours prelude the reappearance of the Sylphs who alone are refined enough to possess the scene, although more evanescent even than it.

> Soft o'er the Shrouds Aerial Whispers breath,
> That seem'd but *Zephyrs* to the Train beneath.
> Some to the Sun their Insect-Wings unfold,
> Waft on the Breeze, or sink in Clouds of Gold.
> Transparent Forms, too fine for mortal Sight,
> Their fluid Bodies half dissolv'd in Light.
> Loose to the Wind their airy Garments flew,
> Thin glitt'ring Textures of the filmy Dew;
> Dipt in the richest Tincture of the Skies,
> Where Light disports in ever-mingling Dies,
> While ev'ry Beam new transient Colours flings,
> Colours that change when'er they wave their Wings.
> (2.59–70; 1714)

The vision is more than enchanting; it is weirdly seductive too—partly *because* it cannot bear the lightest touch of grosser things. As the Sylphs half reveal their fluid bodies, whisper overhead, "loose" their garments, or sink in pleasures where no mortal can follow, they eerily, fastidiously tantalize human sense. For, like the language of the barge scene, they palpitate with "romantic" feelings. Of a highly specialized sort. From their vantage point where they sport and flutter they watch over the purity of melting Maids; but purity as they value it is no very virginal state.

> Know further yet; Whoever fair and chaste
> Rejects Mankind, is by some *Sylph* embrac'd:
> For Spirits, freed from mortal Laws, with ease
> Assume what Sexes and what Shapes they please.
> (1.67–70; 1714)

Ariel's phrasing already hints at the unearthly perversions of sylphic love. Soon he takes open pleasure in the corruptions practised on womankind by his cousin Gnomes.

> 'Tis these that early taint the Female Soul,
> Instruct the Eyes of young *Coquettes* to roll,
> Teach Infants Cheeks a bidden Blush to know,
> And little Hearts to flutter at a *Beau*.
>
> (1.87–90; 1714)

Yet the full force of his offer to Belinda is not felt until we have discovered the alarming fact that the language of ardour and that of false romantic frigidity are, or can be, the same. It is like the dilemma Empson summarizes in his chapter on double-plots: "Everything spiritual and valuable has a . . . revolting parody, very similar to it, with the same name. Only unremitting judgement can distinguish between them." With Belinda, secure in her painted Vessel and smiling on all to the accompaniment of "melting," "dying" sounds, the problem is not just, Will she be gained by the Baron? but the more complex issue, Will she yield to any earthly lover, or is her heart reserved for a simulacrum of love: the sterile coquetries of Sylphs?

IV

That the Sylphs have already won far-reaching victories is evident from the stylizations of fashionable life itself. Passages which in 1712 read as entertaining mock-heroic assume a more sinister fascination in the later versions with virtually no word changed. So whereas the following had been an easy jest at would-be epic's exaggerations—

> For lo! the Board with Cups and Spoons is crown'd,
> The Berries crackle, and the Mill turns round.
> On shining Altars of *Japan* they raise
> The silver Lamp, and fiery Spirits blaze,
> From silver Spouts the grateful Liquors glide,
> And *China's* Earth receives the smoking Tyde.
>
> (3.105–10; 1714, cf. 1.89–94; 1712)

—arriving at the passage in its new context it makes sense to ask (as it hardly did before), What consciousness is registering the physicalities of social life in so acute a way? In 1712 to speak of a cup as "*China's* Earth" was a joke relished for its own sake. But now the shift of scale is full of purpose. For sylphic delicacy is amazed at the grossness of porcelain, endangered (comically) by coffee-floods, and aware that those "fiery Spirits" which promote new stratagems in the Baron's brain may, on inspection, turn out to be sister Termagants after all. The verse quivers with this sylphic sense of things. Yet the Sylphs are not the only ones abnormally responsive to the physical world, and thus over-ready to idolize or fear it. Rather, *their* sensibility blends into the fine textures of fashionable life, and into the consciousness of its inhabitants—as in the next lines, added of course when the poem was recomposed:

> Strait hover round the Fair her Airy Band;
> Some, as she sip'd, the fuming Liquor fann'd,
> Some o'er her Lap their careful Plumes display'd,
> Trembling, and conscious of the rich Brocade.
> (3.113–16; 1714)

The "careful" gestures—hovering, sipping, fanning—are divided between belle and Sylphs, each mimicking the other, as it were. The graces of civilization, which make it so rich and beautiful a thing, have as their parody a conscious simpering niceness. Unregenerate fact is not good enough for these refined creatures—the cultivated beauties *or* the disembodied Sylphs.

Yet even that does not put it strongly enough. The more we register the physical world through the aerial consciousness of Sylphs, the more tantalizingly desirable fineness of beauty seems. But to maintain the exquisite purity which Sylphs admire is a torment to nature; and we feel the strain in the Sylphs' own characteristic motion, "trembling" and "flutt'ring" in restless ecstasies of care. Like the belle, they guard painfully ephemeral beauties: frail china jars, honour, the flirt of a fan or down of powder on a cheek. One does not need to threaten such creatures; the very refinement they value is perilous enough—liable to look like nature racked to a nicety of form. For how can such beauty last? Is it even endurable, when it depends on perfection being kept intact? so that the Sylphs' commission is to ensure the Fair as frivolously uncommitted as themselves.

> Whatever Spirit, careless of his Charge,
> His Post neglects, or leaves the Fair at large,
> Shall feel sharp Vengeance soon o'ertake his Sins,
> Be stopt in *Vials*, or transfixt with *Pins;*
> Or plung'd in Lakes of bitter *Washes* lie,
> Or wedg'd whole Ages in a *Bodkin's* Eye:
> *Gums* and *Pomatums* shall his Flight restrain,
> While clog'd he beats his silken Wings in vain;

Or Alom-*Stypticks* with contracting Power
Shrink his thin Essence like a rivel'd Flower.
(2.125–34; 1714)

Cosmetics as a brutal menace are funny in their way, but there is a strange sexual foreboding here as, on behalf of the human beauties as well as the Sylphs, the wit feels out the sensitive points of spirit-body where ruin can enter it. Transfixed with pain, stopped up, over-flooded, its softness shrunk and damaged: real dangers lie in wait if sylphids sin by leaving humanity "at large." Therefore propriety is revenged when all the artifices which should aid frivolity are used to disable flightiness, natural expression of coquettes, even after death. What anguished imprisonment of body and fluttering spirit together is rendered by those verbs, "plung'd," "clog'd," "wedg'd." Whether we look from the human viewpoint or the Sylphs', the freedom of each form of life to be itself is tyranny over the other.

Yet each in a way needs its tyrant. Without the Sylphs, Belinda would be less magical than she is—that much is clear from the *Locke* of 1712. Without *her* living frailty on the other hand, the Sylphs would have nothing so precious to exercise upon. The deeper we move into the work, the more poignant these interrelations become, and the richer the irony Pope commands. His attention broadens masterfully; wherever he turns in the completed poem, he perceives the contradictions of its social world with a sympathy increasingly sharp, and wittily humane.

Even as originally conceived, Hampton Court demanded more than lightness from him. It lets a glimpse of a larger, more disturbing world into the poem.

Hither our Nymphs and Heroes did resort,
To taste awhile the Pleasures of a Court;
In various Talk the chearful hours they past,
Of, who was *Bitt,* or who *Capotted* last:
This speaks the Glory of the *British Queen,*
And that describes a charming *Indian Screen;*
A third interprets Motions, Looks, and Eyes;
At ev'ry Word a Reputation dies.
Snuff, or the *Fan,* supply each Pause of Chatt,
With singing, laughing, ogling, and all that.
Now, when declining from the Noon of Day,
The Sun obliquely shoots his burning Ray;
When hungry Judges soon the Sentence sign,
And Wretches hang that Jury-men may Dine;

When Merchants from th'Exchange return in Peace,
And the long Labours of the *Toilette* cease—
The Board's with Cups and Spoons, alternate, crown'd;
The Berries crackle, and the Mill turns round.
(1.73–90; 1712)

The passage is a striking one; all the more so for the bitterly simple irony it yields. Admittedly the lines contrast the gossips and the gallows (aristocrats are safely remote from the violence outside) while simultaneously yoking them together (Nymphs brutally indifferent as hanging Judges). But by placing the passage neatly between great Anna's tea-taking just before, and the Statesman's coffee just after, Pope reduces this to a manageable pattern of shock. Each appetite, it turns out, can be measured against another: hungry Judges' against starvelings', and both of them against the thirst fine gentlemen have to "taste awhile" the pleasures of a Court. Intense as it may be, the satiric gaze travels evenly all the way from the Queen to the Wretches over whom she rules.

But when Pope reimagined his poem in 1714 simple ironies were transformed to complex ones. The first sign is the splendid deepening of tone, as easy jokes ("Of, who was *Bitt* or who *Capotted*") disappear, and a new rhythm announces a rich inexorable change of key.

Mean while declining from the Noon of Day,
The Sun obliquely shoots his burning Ray;
The hungry Judges soon the Sentence sign,
And wretches hang that Jury-men may Dine;
The Merchant from th'*Exchange* returns in Peace,
And the long Labours of the *Toilette* cease.
(3.19–24; 1714)

Instead of relying on a "When" to suspend four clauses in turn, heavy with anticipation, the sentence now moves inevitable and calm. Authorial knowingness gives way to a feeling that time surrounds all actions with an equal pressure: "Mean while": an impersonal authority extended over all things, to give dignity to belles and wretches alike. For death may seize one sooner than another, but finally in this long perspective the facts of nature are equidistant from all men, like the sun. Hunger and vanity, selfishness, desperate need, each has its place in the rhythmic procession, as light declines, the felons hang, and the Merchant and the Beauty, freed at last from their labours, can remain at peace. The scale on which we are invited to feel, and the undisturbed spaciousness in which the most incongruous things are set, allows us to realize that even frivolity need not be satirically dismissed. All human facts are capable of grandeur of a kind.

Of course there is no chance we can hold such a vision steady. Ordinary feeling cannot support it, nor indeed can Pope's art, since the same quick searching powers of mind which opened the perspective to us necessarily relinquish it again. But we could hardly wish this otherwise. For the poetry seems to gain strength from recognizing just how elusive the moral order it creates from moment to moment is. No solidified morality could do justice to Belinda's world; and strict justice anyway is the last thing Sylphs would want. *Their* indifference, however, is not freedom so much as a parody of it: a parody of the value Pope can see even in frailty, frivolity, confusion.

> Whether the Nymph shall break *Diana's* Law,
> Or some frail *China* Jar receive a Flaw,
> Or stain her Honour, or her new Brocade,
> Forget her Pray'rs, or miss a Masquerade,
> Or lose her Heart, or Necklace, at a Ball;
> Or whether Heav'n has doom'd that Shock must fall.
> (2.107–12; 1714)

Trivial disasters and real ones are no sooner opposed than their boundaries disappear, leaving a poignancy at this flickering and fading, this merging of values which ought to be distinct. The Sylphs are the shimmering, helpless, half-dissolved guardians of a moral order as flimsy as their own aerial forms. Once such creatures entered the verse, no fixed morality *could* remain. The human viewpoint, the sylphic, the epic sense of things, all play into and out of one another, the limitations of each suggested by the presence alongside it of these contrary possible worlds.

V

It isn't easy to keep all this in balance. The poem is beautiful enough to distract us from the necessary judgments, at the same time as its beauty must be part of whatever judgment we make. But try to formulate the relations of Sylphs to fashionable world, and the choices by which we are faced are disturbing—as the earliest critique of the poem showed. For when the revised *Lock* first appeared (March 1714), six copper engravings accompanied its text, giving visible shape to the impression made on one contemporary at least. And to Du Guernier the engraver the spirits appear as quasi-diabolic imps. In Umbriel's case that is not surprising; but fondling

Belinda on her bed is an incubus-Ariel, surely; while elsewhere too the spirits have a mocking predatory look. Never more so than when, in the guise of *putti,* they surround the girl with their own large baby-faced forms: one trying on her shoes, another tasting her scent bottle, while some shower her with playing cards, hold the glass to focus her difficult cosmetic art, or hover wonderingly beside her funeral urn. In the shadows a belial-cherub lurks; in the foreground another whose legs have openly taken satyr's shape experiments with a mask to cover his horns.

So far as Pope's letters show, he did not commission these engravings himself. On the other hand, his letter of November 2, 1716, sends "inclosed Directions" to the new artist, Gribelin, whose decorative panel for the poem in the large-paper edition of 1717 clearly derives from Du Guernier's old Frontispiece (and Pope's lifelong interest in the sister art of painting suggests how ready he would have been to concern himself with illustrations to his works). Cards, urns, cosmetics, satyrs, and a belle at her looking glass all reappear in a "Hampton Court" setting filled with busy Sylphs. The point is not that the illustrations in every case are so much cruder than the verse; inevitably, they are; but that to conceive, even momentarily, the Sylphs outside the quick light fascinations of that verse brings up decisions of the very kind the Celestials try to keep in abeyance. Having said that, though, the engravings can be allowed to lapse, as Pope allowed them to. Anything they have to offer is already more finely achieved in his verse—and achieved, as the *Rape* moves towards its climax, through a variety of episodes and forms.

Like other readers, Johnson felt some of Pope's means of conveyance could be spared. The second half of the poem might be thought to duplicate effects already obtained. But it seems to me a rather different world is entered with canto 3. After glittering Sylph-induced visions, we come to the weighty matter of cards, and, weightier still, the game which cards enable the characters to play out and, simultaneously, disguise.

> *Belinda* now, whom Thirst of Fame invites,
> Burns to encounter two adventrous Knights,
> At *Ombre* singly to decide their Doom;
> And swells her Breast with Conquests yet to come.
> (3.25–29; 1714)

"Thirst," "Burns," "swells": urgent, if formalized, sexual suggestions initiate the culminating movement of the work.

At first everything is ceremonious, tableau-like; but the game's formality itself overthrows such elegant manners. Within minutes Belinda is set about by warriors and swarthy Moors; Giant Limbs are spread around; bawdy intimations peep from unexpected places ("Puts forth one manly Leg, to sight reveal'd; / The rest his many-colour'd Robe conceal'd"), for the decorum of normal perspective is unsettled: the very care with which the card game is elaborated (never Lilliputian, yet minutely exact—editors explain how you play it) sees to that. So by the time "The Nymph exulting fills with Shouts the Sky," these global reactions have overridden the difference between moral triumph and a game of cards. In Belinda's world anyway the difference is hard to maintain, when Sylphs show an airily equal concern for chastity and for china jars. Thanks to the best efforts of polite society and its perfect "essence," the Sylphs, the very words by which we designate moral choice have been emptied of meaning, until what guards the purity of melting Maids is vanity (if the truth were spoken), "Tho' *Honour* is the Word with Men below." In such a world it is no use appealing to principle, or natural feeling either. Only through feints and rules, as in ombre, society's game, is honest emotion brought into play; but the formality of the game *can* touch it off. Belinda's paleness and excitement, though properly concealed by "Heaps on Heaps" of cards, infuse a live, unsylphic passion into Hampton Court. Committed now, as she never was in the barge scene, her moment of spontaneity frees her, only to expose her to real danger straightaway.

Not that the Baron in himself has serious sexual force. That much was plain when his altar to Love was built out of paper Romances. But as Pope's understanding of his poem grew, so did his power to realize deeper wrongs. In 1714 he still laughed at the sentimental clutter of the sacrifice pile (unchanged since the original *Locke*), and jibed at the Baron's corsets.

> There lay the Sword-knot *Sylvia's* Hands had sown,
> With *Flavia's* Busk that oft had rapp'd his own. . . .
>
> (2.39–40; 1714)

But by 1717 Pope is less indulgent. Sardonically he now picks out the evidence of promiscuities and broken trusts, oddments in odd numbers, whose pathetic incompleteness testifies to the lover's "ardent" Heart:

> There lay three garters, half a pair of gloves;
> And all the trophies of his former loves.
> With tender Billet-doux he lights the pyre,
> And breathes three am'rous sighs to raise the fire.
>
> (2.37–43; 1717)

Adult sexuality always remains beyond him. Even to start with it was coffee that inflamed him to the rape, by sending its modish Vapours to his brain. The Pope of 1712 is startlingly clear about the Baron's action: what it means to him, and to the inhabitants of his society.

> He first expands the glitt'ring *Forfex* wide
> T'inclose the Lock; then joins it, to divide;
> One fatal stroke the sacred Hair does sever
> From the fair Head, for ever, and for ever!
> The living Fires come flashing from her Eyes,
> And Screams of Horrow rend th'affrighted Skies.
> Not louder Shrieks by Dames to Heav'n are cast,
> When Husbands die, or *Lap-dogs* breath their last,
> Or when rich *China* Vessels fal'n from high,
> In glittring Dust and painted Fragments lie!
> (1.115–24; 1712)

In its fashion, masterly. At no point do we reach an easy climax, but register each transition, as the noble sonority of one paragraph ("for ever, and for ever") turns into cheap shrill shrieking in the next. Nor is deflation Pope's only tactic. Rather, satiric reversals are themselves reversed, as the flippancy about Husband-lapdogs modulates into a graver tone: "Or when rich *China* Vessels": perhaps beauty's painted fragments have a sadness after all.

One might have hesitated to suppose Pope could better the passage. But in 1714 he did so, by inserting the Sylphs. They help us feel the cutting of the Lock as real violation—both of Belinda's beauty, and of the code of manners which holds this civilization by fine threads. Graceful and ceremonious, the perfection Belindas achieve is easily lost—which indeed is part of their charm.

> Swift to the Lock a thousand Sprights repair,
> A thousand Wings, by turns, blow back the Hair,
> And thrice they twitch'd the Diamond in her Ear,
> Thrice she look'd back, and thrice the Foe drew near.
> Just in that instant, anxious *Ariel* sought
> The close Recesses of the Virgin's Thought;
> As on the Nosegay in her Breast reclin'd,
> He watch'd th'Ideas rising in her Mind,
> Sudden he view'd, in spite of all her Art,
> An Earthly Lover lurking at her Heart.
> Amaz'd, confus'd, he found his Pow'r expir'd,
> Resign'd to Fate, and with a Sigh retir'd.

> The Peer now spreads the glitt'ring *Forfex* wide,
> T'inclose the Lock; now joins it, to divide.
> Ev'n then, before the Fatal Engine clos'd,
> A wretched *Sylph* too fondly interpos'd;
> Fate urg'd the Sheers, and cut the *Sylph* in twain,
> (But Airy Substance soon unites again)
> The meeting Points the sacred Hair dissever
> From the fair Head, for ever and for ever!
> Then flash'd the living Lightnings from her Eyes,
> And Screams of Horror rend th'affrighted Skies.
> Not louder Shrieks by Dames to Heav'n are cast,
> When Husband's or when Monkeys breath their last.
> (3.135–58; 1714)

The deed is magnified to its most heroical size; but that is appropriate, and not mock-epic indulgence, since this time the doom-filled language really belongs to some of the participants. A deed of these dimensions certainly can disable Sylphs, whose light militia succumbs to punctilio itself (a parallel here to the card game), when a thousand wings "take turns" to disarrange the hair, and even Ariel for all his captaincy is too graceful not to "recline" on the nosegay and capitulate at first glimpse of the Enemy, with a resigning "Sigh." At the catastrophe therefore we shake free of ineffectual Sylphs and return to human actors instead.

But Sylph-consciousness is not so easily laid aside. The longer Pope contemplated his poem the less it seemed possible to disengage polite behaviour from those exquisite perversions of good breeding the Sylphs offer. The two are dismayingly alike. So much so that by 1717 he felt he must add Clarissa's speech, "to open more clearly the MORAL," and coming back to the climactic rape saw nicer distinctions called for there as well. Increase of wit now means increased humanity too.

> Not louder shrieks to pitying heav'n are cast,
> When husbands, or when lapdogs breathe their last;
> Or when rich *China* vessels, fal'n from high,
> In glittering dust, and painted fragments lie!
> (3.156–59; 1717)

The burlesqued "Dames" of 1712 and 1714 vanish, though their shrieks continue to be heard: by a "pitying" Heaven which does not mock in any simple way but listens, tenderly receptive, to the cries mounting up from foolish human kind. And the tightened zeugmatic syntax points where the folly came from: "When husbands, or when lapdogs," the women are practising sylphic equations of things which ought to be kept apart. By identifying the malaise, we resist it; and once we do, the helplessness which mourns dogs, husbands, porcelain, all at once or else in nicely calibrated sequence can be granted its proper pathos. Such detachment, in Sylphs *or* their followers, is pitiable, though very nearly indestructible as well. So the couplets rouse finenesses of sympathy from everything they touch, down to the "glittering" dust of line 159 over which, with its vowel restored, the voice is allowed to hesitate lamentingly. Neither sympathy nor dismissal is good enough. Even the phrase "wretched Sylph" stands midway from petulance ("the wretched thing, it will get in the way") and Miltonic sadness ("what futile suffering presumption brings on itself"). As the Baron's scissors close on Belinda and her guardians, we value what is destroyed as highly as we may; then all at once see the loss as laughably minute. For how much *is* destroyed? The scissors themselves, opening "T'inclose" and joining "to divide," interpret their own action two ways.

One can see with what care Pope worked over the scene, and why such care was needed. His language, its blend of familiarity, grandeur and fastidiousness all sharpened to a tiny point, enables him to draw up meanings which otherwise lie out of sight, too imponderable, or else too gross, for delicate verse to handle. As it is, however, the solemn latinisms are absurd, yet they outline the Baron's every gesture as his "fatal Engine" mimes a sexual act and at the same time substitutes for one. I mean, his rape of course is nothing more than imitation. The irony is that in fashionable life a substitute-rape may be *worse* indeed than a real one: for the Baron violates exactly what can't be secret—the way Belinda looks; whereas sexual acts can be (in every sense) "unknown."

We might call it Thalestris-morality: a code of Appearances, where nothing counts unless seen, and every truth is reduced to the nice (or horrid) "things they say": "And all your Honour in a Whisper lost." It didn't take the final versions of the poem for Pope to uncover this; he had dramatized such pseudomorality in the *Locke* of 1712.

> Oh had the Youth but been content to seize
> Hairs less in sight—or any Hairs but these!
> Gods! shall the Ravisher display this Hair,
> While the Fops envy, and the Ladies stare!
> *Honour* forbid! at whose unrival'd Shrine
> Ease, Pleasure, Virtue, All, our Sex resign.
> (2.19–24; 1712)

The shameful ease of the declension can tempt the prude (shaking her head to hear of Pleasure's name) as well as the libertine. For to this idol *Honour* women sacrifice the honour they really have, chaste Virtue, until by a series of self-undoing puns the language of "purity" is turned inside out to reveal a morality antisexual indeed, being frigid and promiscuous both at once. All this is already present in the *Locke*. What Pope did in 1714 was to body it forth in a new drama, not of Lovers and Ladies only, but of Sylphs, as his wittily exact Dedication declares:

> For they say, any Mortals may enjoy the most intimate Familiarities with these gentle Spirits, upon a Condition very easie to all true *Adepts,* an inviolate preservation of Chastity

—"the most intimate Familiarities," with the sole proviso that real sexuality is foresworn. That indeed is the libidinous "Chastity" you embrace in embracing Sylphs: a mock-virginity from which the spirits of "Honour" can never break themselves. All is Appearance, maintained by flawless ego in a travesty of authentic self-venturing and self-possession. Hence Ariel's command, "Thy own Importance know." Yet narcissistic, titillating, though the Sylphs may be, they turn the falsity to magic of a kind. Aloft in the poem's own crystal wilds of air, they give a new dimension to human lives, and new comedy by which those lives are beautified and judged.

To say that a sexual drama runs through the poem is true enough, then, in an abstract summary way. Pope does examine genteel society and Belinda's development (or failure to develop) as a woman. But where we conceptualize, he makes real the shimmering sensuous fragility of the Sylphs: not as a covering myth which adroit readers must prize off to get to the "real" concerns, but as *itself* the other side to darker forces. Almost literally so. For Belinda's world through cantos 1 to 3 is registered as surfaces: looking glass, silver Thames, flat playing cards, light sparkling on objects, reflected as sheen or lustre, or glittering in films of air. Not until canto 4 does its underside appear. In the Cave of Spleen, however, is summoned up a darkened, hollowed world, thick with vapours, dreams, conscious forms of voluble aching emptiness. Here are windy bags, sighing Jars and calling Bottles. Obviously (too obviously, perhaps, for all the elegance of wit) this is the realm of Uterus, and of what etymology proclaims is its "hysteric" power.

> Hail wayward Queen;
> Who rule the Sex to Fifty from Fifteen,
> Parent of Vapors and Female Wit,
> Who give th'*Hysteric* or *Poetic* Fit.
>
> (4.57–60; 1714)

But the uterus rules not only women; sexual nature in them, satisfied or distorted, affects us all. And Pope's wit goes deeper; to associate these distortions with the very refinements (poetry, etc.) civilized living applauds. That, and not a simpler point about "frustration," is what the Cave reveals. For in one creative act the valuable and degrading are fused: art, religion, manners, all momentarily sink back to baseness as though by some entropic law. Poetic and hysteric fit are equally available, *each* one a parody of the other; "Men prove with Child, as pow'rful Fancy works"; while as for the godly, pettishness and prayer are indistinguishable.

The implications of all this have been teased out often enough. Art and Neurosis, civilization and its discontents—such interpretations of the Cave are unavoidable this century, I suppose. Yet they don't suggest how imaginative Pope is in his audacities, how unprogrammatic in short. Nor do they remind us that the ironies of Spleen continue to the end. For the Goddess fills her wondrous bag with a full supply of current affectations, sighs, sobs, Passions, and the rest; yet up from the nether realm comes the one thing—outrage—by which perverted nature might after all be healed.

To bring release out of affectation took Pope some time. His first presentation of Belinda's grief was inclined to burlesque her.

> But see! the *Nymph* in Sorrow's Pomp appears,
> Her eyes half languishing, half drown'd in Tears;
> Now livid pale her Cheeks, now glowing red.
> (2.59–61; 1712)

By 1714, however, she contrives to be touching just because she is (thanks to the spirits) so stylish. Hers is sorrow in the modern way, the only way she knows; for Umbriel breaks his vial, and

> see! the *Nymph* in beauteous Grief appears,
> Her Eyes half languishing, half drown'd in Tears;
> On her heav'd Bosom hung her drooping Head,
> Which, with a Sigh, she rais'd; and thus she said.
> (4.143–46; 1714)

The performance does not cease to be affected; gracefulness in Belinda's world is always liable to be that; but all Pope's rewritings so far prepare us for the appeal of her (ridiculous) grief. Indeed, the newly tender cadence of the lines prompts us to realize that, just as there is a sense in which she awaits the Baron, tempting him to rape (the conscious smoothness of that bended neck exposing the delicious curls), so likewise when he's accomplished the deed her dismay is not that he's done so much, but that he has not done more. Aided by graces Umbriel supplies, her indignation invites a further, more genuine assault.

> See the poor remnants of these slighted hairs!
> My hands shall rend what ev'n thy rapine spares:
> These, in two sable ringlets taught to break,
> Once gave new beauties to the snowy neck;
> This sister-lock now sits uncouth, alone,
> And in its fellow's fate foresees its own;
> Uncurl'd it hangs, the fatal sheers demands;
> And tempts once more thy sacrilegious hands.
> Oh hadst thou, cruel! been content to seize
> Hairs less in sight, or any hairs but these!
> (4.167–76; 1717)

The lines, originally given to Thalestris, are only *just* polite enough to lie within Belinda's range; and that she speaks them shows how little she pretends to smiling indifference now. She draws all eyes, as by a verbal blush, to the tempting other Hairs. But that is because her indignation has, only, worldy knowing forms to take. So her half-innocent heroics shade into *double-entendre* (1717 actually introduces the word "rapine"). Thus sylphic values have not exactly been discarded; rather, they *contribute* to Belinda's finally unsylphic appeal. And that, with all its implications, is central to the poem, I think. For to the end we never know how far she is actually set free. To be sure, she is no mere coquette. Even at her dressing table she is a living beauty. And at the moment of climax Ariel finds an earthly lover lurking at her heart, where pure sylphic frigidity should be. So the Sylphs are obliged to retire, leaving the mortals to battle for themselves. But ("see how oft Ambitious Aims are cross'd") the outcome of the battle is unclear. The Lock is lost, yet gained by no earthly lover; Belinda's marred beauty is not repaired by beauty of a deeper kind, since to take up her role as Woman she must lose that of Virgin first, and this in Pope's poem we never see her do. For one thing, it wouldn't be proper. Instead, we see her enlist more firmly in the Amazonian values of her world, and thus earn Clarissa's famous warning against "Flights and Screams and Scolding." It is a timely rebuke; for Belinda retreats from womanliness, it seems, to defend the injured vanity of the unmaturing belle; and compared with those airs, Clarissa's speech does sound like "the MORAL" of the poem.

> Oh! if to dance all night, and dress all day,
> Charm'd the small-pox, or chas'd old age away;

> Who would not scorn what huswife's cares produce,
> Or who would learn one earthly thing of use?
> To patch, nay ogle, might become a Saint,
> Nor could it sure be such a sin to paint.
> But since, alas! frail beauty must decay,
> Curl'd or uncurl'd, since Locks will turn to grey,
> Since painted, or not painted, all shall fade,
> And she who scorns a man, must die a maid;
> What then remains, but well our Pow'r to use,
> And keep good Humour still whate'er we lose?
> (5.19–30, 1717)

After such a speech is it not a mark of Belinda's shallowness that she frowns, and, worse still, takes arms with Thalestris?

Though I would once have said so, Pope's discrimination is, I now think, more subtle. For he detects the taint of high-minded insincerity in Clarissa's overconscious speech: the cosy touches ("to patch, nay ogle"), the unctuous advice, to "trust me, Dear! good Humour can prevail." If Belinda must accept the alternatives, of scorning a man or dying a maid, it is not on these self-satisfied terms. They bring us close to poignant realizations, then substitute new falsity in place of old. So as against Clarissa's campaign of smiling well-used "Pow'r," the termagant anger to which Belinda gives way turns out to be honest, life-engaging after all.

> See fierce *Belinda* on the Baron flies,
> With more than usual lightning in her eyes:
> Nor fear'd the Chief th'unequal flight to try,
> Who sought no more than on his foe to die.
> (5.75–78; 1717)

No doubt a Belinda freed from "social" values altogether would satisfy us more. Pope doesn't allow that, though. Too intelligent to imagine that liberation ever comes except on terms that society itself provides, he sees Belinda's selfhood to some extent set free, but always as the selfhood of one society rather than another. Yet here the poem's finest paradoxes appear. The way into freedom is for Belinda to act upon the forms and frivolities, even the bad-humoured ones, her society provides. And in doing so, a kind of reality is achieved. It isn't perfect; it involves silliness, temper, vanity, and so on; and the ultimate fate of the belle—fulfilment, or bitter old age—still remains unknown. But not even the sylphic Essences of society ever achieve much more. Like Belinda's, their beauty is would-be perfect, but actually tremulous and troubled—which, far from being a defect, increases beauty the more. Indeed, their fluttering anxious guardianship heightens the vulnerability, hence preciousness, of whatever they guard.

> Some o'er her Lap their careful Plumes display'd,
> Trembling, and conscious of the rich Brocade.

Such protection invites disaster; so too the outrage of the belle; but in either case that is almost the highest compliment Pope can pay. For it enables him to show his heroine a woman after all, and there is a triumphant sadness in his apotheosis-tribute to her mortal frailty.

> When those fair suns shall set, as set they must,
> And all those tresses shall be laid in dust;
> This Lock, the Muse shall consecrate to fame,
> And midst the stars inscribe *Belinda's* name!
> (5.147–50; 1717)

Only if the hair is ravished can Belinda gain "new glory," and only if she is laid in dust can Pope immortalize her in the "shining sphere," the civilization, of his verse.

VI

Immortality poems are not what we think of as his province, but he strove to give his verses at least such permanence as art may have. Unlike the quick-fading effusions of scribblers and critics, they last, with a lastingness secured by every scrupulosity of rewriting. Indeed, Pope's genius is strong enough to delight in the very things which resist immortalizing: nonsense precipitate like running lead, momentary monsters that rise and fall—it is a positive pleasure to bring them, too, into the couplet's order. The more highly finished his art, in fact, the readier it seems to catch things which have no permanence at all: transitory, unfinalized things. The ephemeral always fascinated him, and his interest in the women of fashionable life is surely part of this. For the beauty of the Belle, by its nature, cannot endure. All such beauty, and hers especially, becomes a ghost of what it was, at the end of Moral Essay 2 still desolatingly in motion. The very graces by which she heightens her appeal, and the artifice which would camouflage decline, show how precariously she reigns. So it is not surprising such figures attract a curious play of feeling as Pope contemplates their careers: indignation, shocked disgust, a darting tender fondness. They occasion some of his greatest poetry, from the *Locke* of 1712 to the great antitype of the belle, Queen Dulness herself, gross, grave, laborious, busy, bold and blind, and gauzily be-fogged or tinselled o'er in varying fool's colours. But *The Dunciad* claims attention on its own. More to the point are the women of the "social" poems: the two epistles to Miss Blount, or (still more) the Moral Essays, work of an older poet prepared to admit a violence his earlier celebrations hardly show. For there *is* an idealizing strain in *The Rape of the Lock:* to incorporate it was necessary to Pope's critique of that world; whereas the Moral Essays tackle not just society as it might wish to appear, but sprawling energies of a far more savage kind. Even the deathbed scenes of epistle 1, or Pope's vision of a femaleness in, of all things, money itself (epistle 3), cannot match the portraits of the second essay: Narcissa, Flavia, Atossa and the rest, not shielded by pathos like earlier Unfortunate Ladies ("Life's idle business at one gasp be o'er"); on the contrary, the unpathetic now becomes a positive Popean strength as he contemplates their appetites and habits, coupling

> Sappho at her toilet's greazy task,
> With Sappho fragrant at an ev'ning Mask:
> So morning Insects that in muck begun,
> Shine, buzz, and fly-blow in the setting-sun.
>
> (*Epistle 2, To a Lady, Of the Characters of Women,* 2.25–28)

Disgust and revulsion are strong; but so too is the sheer vitality of these insects whose inhuman processes are not just to be shuddered from. If anything, their life cycle, from its start in muck to its self-regenerating end, prompts wonder at its being so rapid and complete—prompts delight indeed (witness that attractive "Shine"), and this ambivalence transfers itself back to Sappho, so that the first couplet's cruel antithesis is turned by the second into a metamorphosis natural as insects' under a setting sun.

Yet, characteristic of the Moral Essays, these transformations are caught in a single sentence and the arc of a single day. Belinda at *her* dressing table is not summed up in any such vignette or left like Sappho in two dire couplets finished and transfixed. Of course, considering the appetites with which the second epistle deals, one can see why its episodes detach themselves into a row of portraits. The rebellious warring energies of these women, the ferocity of their demands on life, defeat all attempts to set them in a poetic-moral order—particularly the attempts of a little, laughed-at gallant like Pope. It is a more confident impulse that carries Belinda out into her world, to surround her with Sylphs and launch her on the silver Thames. Now, in the midst of polite society, Pope's landscapes, Nymphs,

Swains, elementals, evoke a pastoral freedom. We glimpse (if only glimpse) an innocence older than Christianity, in the vision of Arcadia and "*Diana's Law.*" Unlike the Moral Essays, and like no other poem he wrote, this has the shape of myth. But in the end it is clear that no myth was capable of holding Augustan idealism and reality together. By the time of *The Dunciad* there was no epic unity eighteenth-century England could sustain in the imagination of its greatest writer; and if *The Rape of the Lock* suggests there might have been, it can do so only because it encloses itself in its own world perfectly. It does not require the praise of modern criticism, that it is or that it sustains a poetic myth.

Rather, if we follow where the poetry itself is at its most vital and engaged, we come almost always to Belinda and her Sylphs. In imagining them, Pope's touch is exquisitely fine. Nowhere else I know of does he so movingly evoke the promise, and vulnerability, of woman's nature. So this, more than his epistles to Miss Blount, is a love poem I want to say, though of a strange and beautiful remoteness. "Strange," because it is addressed only to a Belinda, who lives (only) in the art of the poet himself. Nevertheless a love poem is one of the things it is. But then, resemblances, echoes of all kinds, live fleetingly in the verse, and to feel their momentary pressure is enough. For in this poem, so much revised and altered, we see Pope come to realize that amongst the things we value lastingly is mutability itself.

A World of Artefacts: *The Rape of the Lock* as Social History

C. E. Nicholson

When Geoffrey Tillotson, in the final paragraph of his introduction to the "Twickenham" edition of *The Rape of the Lock,* comments that "the second version is inexhaustible," readers cannot help reflecting upon the fact that generations of commentators on the poem as well as the detailed annotations offered editorially by Tillotson himself conspire to undermine his remark. Indeed the wealth of scholarship revealed by those annotations demonstrates conclusively that almost every line in *The Rape* echoes, parodies, adapts or rephrases moments of a literary tradition reaching from the Bible to the reign of Queen Anne. Pope's wholehearted devotion to the formal excellence of his verse is evinced in the poem's marvellous ability to carry within itself both a deep respect for, and also a jester's irreverence towards, patterns of poetry that are normally taken to be standards of Classical elegance. And yet this formal ambivalence of the mock-heroic genre, as Pope manipulates it, has received scant critical attention. Similarly, although a wide range of Pope's work has been examined for the light it sheds upon shifting patterns of social, personal, and political behaviour during the period in which he lived, *The Rape of the Lock* has usually been accepted as a relatively superficial treatment of his society, as "the mock-epic of a mock-world, the make-believe celebration of a society of play-actors." Even Geoffrey Tillotson expresses a kind of doubt when he writes that "though no reader can fail to be 'conscious of the rich Brocade' of the 1714 version, the story itself is not so proportionate in 1714 as in 1711."

What seems to have escaped attention is the possibility that in the 1714

From *Literature and History* 5, no. 2 (Autumn 1979).

version of *The Rape,* the story itself has changed and that the thin thread of the incident between Lord Petre and Arabella Fermor is woven into a complex design in which the youthful poet undertakes a light-hearted but nonetheless profound and far-reaching examination of what was happening to a particular section of his England. He felt able, in a letter to the Marriot ladies, to describe the five-canto version as "a pretty complete picture of the life of our modern ladies in this idle town," and the nature of the expansions upon the earlier version registers much more than simply a desire to produce a more polished and sophisticated example of a mock-epic poem. One literary critic has paid serious attention to the underlying themes explored by Pope: Ralph Cohen rightly insists that "in *The Rape of the Lock* change must be interpreted in terms of natural or normal change and unnatural or artificial and grotesque change." Social and economic historians of the period offer convincing evidence in support of such an approach to the poem, and it will be useful to glance briefly at what some of them have to say about the social milieu from which the poem sprang, as well as to glance at literary parallels to provide a context and a sense of contemporary consciousness wider than the immediate issues that gave the poem its first birth.

In his book *The Financial Revolution,* P. G. M. Dickson descibes the effects of what he calls the process of "building up the [financial] infrastructure of the industrial revolution," a process whereby an entirely new system of finance rapidly changed the basis upon which government organised both itself and its national responsibilities. "The economic effects of government borrowing on the landed interest were discussed primarily in terms of social prejudice. . . . On the other hand, the effects of the Financial Revolution were discussed in largely economic terms, for trade was increasingly accepted as the motor that drove the whole economy." To a student of the literature of the period such a remark might appear to have more relevance to the writings of Swift or Defoe, or perhaps to Pope's "Epistle to Bathurst" with its hilarious attack upon the notion of paper credit. But if such a student is prepared to listen to other historians, then Pope's interior design in *The Rape of the Lock* might begin to reveal itself. And in this respect, J. G. A. Pocock's *The Machiavellian Moment* is a work that should form part of any bibliography seeking to assist students of Augustan literature. It should, for example, make no unwarrantable demand upon such readers to accept that "the half-century following the revolution of 1688 . . . was the era in which political thought became engrossed with the conscious recognition of change in the economic and social foundations of politics and the political personality, so that the *zoon politikon* took on his modern character of participant observer in processes of material and historical change fundamentally affecting his nature." But Pope's affectionately indulgent attitude towards the "beau-monde" of Queen Anne's reign together with his sheer delight in satirizing London's fashionable society might continue to persuade some that *The Rape* is nothing more than a piece of light-hearted raillery. So perhaps another remark made by Pocock might provide the necessary corrective: "an anatomy of the great debate between the 'landed' and 'monied' interests, conducted by the journalists and publicists of Queen Anne's reign, reveals that there were no pure dogmas or simple antitheses, and few assumptions that were not shared and employed to differing purposes by the writers of either side." The ambivalence of comic surface and the deeper implications of Pope's poem suggests a ready poetic analogy for Pocock's comment.

From the wealth of possibilities that the period presents, one literary parallel should prove helpful. If we remember that five years after the complete version of *The Rape* appeared, *Robinson Crusoe* was first published, and three years after that *Moll Flanders* was for sale, a common factor (and perhaps the pun is in this instance permissible) begins to emerge. Dorothy Van Ghent, in her study *The English Novel: Form and Function,* makes the following observation,

> We notice, for instance, that Moll's world contains many things—tangible things such as watches and wigs and yardage and goods and necklaces and dresses and barrels and bales and bottles and trunks . . . In *Moll* there is a relatively great frequency in the naming of that kind of object which constitutes material wealth . . . Schematically what has been happening here is the conversion of all subjective, emotional and moral experience—implicit in the fact of Moll's five years of marriage and motherhood—into pocket and bank money, into the materially measurable.

Compare that with Tillotson's acknowledgement that "the epic is thingless beside Pope's poem with its close-packed material objects"; and a literary-historical link suggests itself.

Of course a gulf of social class separates Moll from Belinda, but in a more abiding sense they both inhabit a world whose values are fundamentally similar, and it can even be argued that an apparent social separation had, anyway, a topographical foundation since "London was a double town. One end was a royal and parliamentary capital, governed, so far as it had a government, by an obscure condominium of palace officials and nominees of the Dean and chapter of Westminster. The other was virtually a mercantile republic." And when Pope, in the letter to the Marriot ladies quoted earlier, reflects upon the fact that "people who would rather [*The Rape*] were let alone laugh at it, and seem heartily merrily, at the same time that they are uneasy"; we are tempted to wonder whether the cause of that uneasy laughter might not be rooted in an unwilling recognition that the Molls and the Belindas of the period differed not at all in kind but only in degree. The degree, of course, is crucial. It accounts for the wit and grace with which Pope embellishes his perception of the times. Though even here it might be worth suggesting that his "rich Brocade" as well as his superb parody of epic style, are themselves indications of ambivalent yearnings for what Pocock calls "a classically cognizable history and a classically cognizable society, neither of which is to be expected in a universe of mobile credit and expectation." So, when Dorothy Van Ghent notices that "these tangible, material objects with which Moll is so deeply concerned, are not at all vivid in texture," she is indicating the different styles which present these two archetypes of fictive women, since the opposite is true of the luminous, vibrant things that compose Belinda's universe.

If, then, "in both his career and his writing Defoe embodied the projecting spirit of self-interest, avarice, and individualism," Pope can, with equal accuracy be seen to reach more deeply into the psychological effects of such motivation. For although Moll Flanders expends her spirit in a materialist pursuit, she does at least possess a combative kind of initiative. In contrast, Belinda has receded into a relative passivity. Moll's vigorous scramble for commodities is transformed, in Belinda's couplet-world of ease and elegance into a fetishised sexuality, so that the "thinghood" which Moll sees as the index of success enters Belinda's soul and recreates that soul in its own image. Belinda, recognizable as the classic portrait of woman in the new rentier class, becomes an object of voyeurism not only for others, but in her own eyes also.

The very title of *The Rape of the Lock* registers the remoteness of authentic human relationships from the fetishised consciousness of Belinda's existence, and practically every couplet in the poem infers unnatural connections between social life and the world of objects, systematically and ingeniously suggesting the ways in which human life is "lived" by means of an extension into the objects that gradually form the subject of the poem. It is the "trivial Things" which operate in the world Pope creates and human capacities are correspondingly diminished. The famous line from the equally famous toilet scene, "Puffs, Powders, Patches, Bibles, Billet-doux" (1.138) is only the most obvious example of the pervasive displacement of values explored by the poem, for if, as Pocock suggests, "money and credit had indeed dissolved the social frame into a shifting mobility of objects that were desired and fictions that were fantasized about," then such a collapse of traditional religious significance is appropriate. And the same point can be made about the couplet "On her white Breast a sparkling *Cross* she wore, / Which *Jews* might kiss, and Infidels adore" (2.7–8), where the italics are only the first sign of dislocated values, but also where the epithet "sparkling," harking back as it does to the "glitt'ring Spoil" with which Belinda has just been decked, further suppresses any specifically Christian connotations adhering to the image of crucifixion, reducing the cross to an item of jewellery and equating its power with Belinda's breast, after either of which Jew or Infidel may "legitimately" lust.

In this giddy world of gilded chariots, garters and stars, it is hardly surprising that a deep-rooted reaction should take place:

> With Varying Vanities, from ev'ry Part,
> They shift the moving Toyshop of their Heart;
> Where Wigs with Wigs, with Sword-knots Sword-knots
> strive,
> Beaus banish Beaus, and Coaches Coaches drive.
> (1.99–102)

The heart itself has become the production centre of a kind of puppet-life. But what is happening here is more than simply the proliferation of objects. Rather it is the expropriation by the objects of human motivation, the assumption by the nonhuman of human characteristics, so that the human residue, the beaus, and the aural pun is emphatic, becomes inseparable from, because identified through, the objects which clutter not only their physical universe but also their spiritual being. The difficulty of actually reading the third line quoted is apt, and the interpenetration of human and nonhuman is consistently developed so that by the time we read "But now secure the painted Vessel glides" (2.47), we have little idea whether Belinda or her boat is being described.

II

What is being suggested is that *The Rape of the Lock* provides a poetic grammar for the process whereby relations between people acquire the characteristics of being relations between things, a process during which commodities acquire an autonomy which conceals their true nature. More than a hundred years later, Karl Marx found it difficult to express the theory of this movement towards reification, and it is a tribute to the extraordinary perceptiveness displayed by Pope that a comment by Marx can be adapted to account for the function of the sylphs. Marx writes,

> A commodity appears, at first sight, a very trivial thing, and easily understood. Its analysis shows that it is, in reality, a very queer thing, abounding in metaphysical subleties and theological niceties . . . In order that these objects may enter into relation with each other . . . their guardians must place themselves in relation to one another, as persons whose will resides in those objects, and must behave in such a way that each does not appropriate the commodity of the other, and part with his own, except by means of an act done by mutual consent.

Accordingly, in Pope's scheme of things, the deities of the poem are named after objects, they attend to the objects which name them and, at the moment of appropriation, they are as ineffectual in their task "in air," as the notion of honour is inoperative in the mundane realm. Certainly the sylphs, as object-spirits in an object-world, cannot protect Belida herself. The elaborate fiction of their particularised domain collapses when she succumbs, "in spite of all her Art," to the natural occurrence of sexual desire (3.143). Until that point, sexuality is repressed, attenuated, fetishised—a surrogate performance as in the game of Ombre, or a fantasy of erotic substitutionism, as in the Baron's need for the trophy of the lock of hair itself.

The famous toilet scene which closes the first canto can be seen to derive its significance from the dehumanising process that characterizes the poem as a whole, for when Belinda "intent adores / With Head uncover'd, the *Cosmetic* Pow'rs" (1.123–24) she is in fact idolizing herself through the medium of the objects which will transform her appearance, which will "create" her public image. There is only one Belinda, but the mirror reflexion conveys to the reader precisely the reified image that is the object of all her devotions. And again the cosmetic paraphernalia surrounding Belinda rises to an active presence, as she surrenders herself to them; a casket "unlocks" its jewels, perfume "breathes," and "Files of Pins" transitively extend themselves. Finally an abstraction, "awful Beauty," assumes command and presides over the contrived dawn of Belinda's attractions. And in the second canto, Pope's precise use of reificatory zeugma reveals his own awareness of the radical dislocations embodied in Belinda:

> Whether the Nymph shall break Diana's Law,
> Or some frail *China* Jar receive a Flaw,
> Or stain her Honour, or her new Brocade,

Forget her Pray'rs, or miss a Masquerade,
Or lose her Heart, or Necklace, at a Ball.
(2.105–9)

It has already been seen that the heart, in this poem, reproduces the values of objects, and Pope's placing of these lines immediately before the naming of the deities points to his awareness. For beneath its fluently contrived surface structure, *The Rape of the Lock* charts with hilarious accuracy the historical advent of a form of social organisation of men wherein, as Marx comments, "their own social action takes the form of the action of objects, which rule the producers instead of being ruled by them," so that human behaviour, and the values it constructs appear to be not the productions of human activity at all, but "laws of nature" imposed from outside. Or, as the poem slyly puts it, " 'Tis but their *Sylph,* the wise Celestials know, / Though *Honour* is the Word with Men below" (1.77–78).

Pope is at pains to indicate the pervasiveness of this quality of life, and the third canto opens with just such an extension of the area of the poem's concern, introducing statesmanship as the equivalent of sexual horse trading, and regard for monarchy as the equivalent of admiration for filigree woodwork. But more significantly, there follow the lines that for one critic of the poem represent a "momentary glimpse of the world of serious affairs, of the world of business and law . . . an echo of the 'real' world":

Meanwhile declining from the Noon of Day,
The Sun obliquely shoots his burning Ray;
The hungry Judges soon the Sentence sign,
And Wretches hang that Jury-men may Dine;
The Merchant from th'*Exchange* returns in Peace,
And the long Labours of the *Toilette* cease.
(3.19–24)

It may seem odd to seek a separation at this juncture between Belinda's world, and another, "glimpsed" here, which somehow exists outside it, and the comic perversion of values is in any case characteristic. But the essential unity of vision, the underlying link between the apparent brutality here and the seeming frivolity everywhere else, is again suggested by Pope's conflating use of italics.

The scramble for commodities which defines a Moll Flanders as "economic woman" is strictly equated with Belinda's adoration for the objects of her dressing table, and Pope's earliest readers would have had little difficulty in recognising the equation being made, since the architectural design of the Royal Exchange gave immediate point to the couplet. A contemporary description runs, "Above stairs there are *Walks,* with near 200 Shops, full of choice Commodities, especially for Mens and Womens Apparel, besides other *Shops* below the portico." There is in fact further evidence to suggest that Pope was perfectly aware of the correspondence being made in these two lines. Twelve months before the first verion of *The Rape* appeared in Lintot's *Miscellany* Addison published an essay as *Spectator 69* in which he confessed himself ravished by the prospect of a busy day at the Royal Exchange and which provides a useful gloss for significant elements in *The Rape of the Lock*—indeed, at certain points in the poem Pope appears to have had Addison's eulogy consciously in mind:

> Almost every *degree* [of traffic] among mankind produces something peculiar to it. The Food often grows in one Country, and the Sauce in another. The Fruits of Portugal are corrected by the Products of *Barbadoes;* the Infusion of a *China* Plant sweetned with the Pith of an *Indian* Cane; the Phillipick Islands give a Flavour to our *European* Bowls. The single Dress of a Woman of Quality is often the Product of an hundred Climates. The Muff and the Fan come together from the different Ends of the Earth. The Scarf is sent from the Torrid Zone, and the Tippet from beneath the Pole. The Brocade Petticoat rises out of the mines of *Peru,* and the Diamond Necklace out of the Bowels of *Indostan.*

Belinda springs irrepressibly to mind as what Addison calls "a kind of Additional Empire" lands in profusion upon her dressing table. And the series of transparent verbal and thematic similarities is continued:

> Nor has Traffic more enriched our Vegetable World, than it has improved the whole Face of Nature among us . . . Our Tables are stored with Spices, and oils, and Wines: Our Rooms are filled with Pyramids of *China,* and adorned with the Workmanship of *Japan.* . . . We repair our Bodies by the Drugs of *America,* and repose ourselves under *Indian* Canopies . . . Traffick . . . supplies us with everything that is Convenient and Ornamental.

What Addison considers to be an improvement, Pope treats more ambivalently as a process of glittering, though nonetheless grotesque, transformations. And in the same essay, Addison blandly asserts what Pope, in the opening lines of the third canto, chooses to leave at the level of satiric suggestion. "Factors in the Trading World are what Ambassadors are in the Politick World: they negotiate Affairs, conclude Treaties, and maintain a good Correspondence between those wealthy Societies of Men that are divided from one another by Seas and Oceans." Pope similarly collapses the distinctions between these two worlds but in high comic spirit:

> Here Britain's Statesmen oft the Fall foredoom
> Of Foreign Tyrants, and of Nymphs at home;
> Here Thou, Great *Anna*! whom three Realms obey,
> Dost sometimes Counsel take—and sometimes *Tea*.
> (3.5–8)

The trader and the politician are one, and the historical accuracy underpinning the satire is now accepted. Carswell, for example, comments that it was "undoubtedly the case that the new class of business men were finding it worth their while to find and occupy seats in Parliament. By 1702 there were at least sixty of them in the Commons."

A glance at Pope's treatment of the new riches celebrated by Addison reveals his more ambiguous attitude, and the comically inflated description of the coffee ritual in canto three is to the point:

> For lo! the Board with Cups and Spoons is crown'd,
> The Berries crackle, and the Mill turns round.
> On Shining Altars of *Japan* they Raise
> The silver Lamp; the fiery spirits blaze.
> From silver Spouts the grateful Liquors glide,
> While *China's* Earth receives the smoking Tyde.
> At once they gratify their Scent and Taste,
> And frequent Cups prolong the rich Repast.
> (3.105–12)

A sense of the marvellous is richly maintained, while subtle ambiguities in grammar are left to make their mark. In a letter to Arbuthnot, dated July 1714, Pope records a scene in which there was "likewise a Side Board of Coffee which the Dean roasted with his own hands in an Engine for the purpose, his landlady attending, all the while that office was performing." The human control over the making of coffee expressed here tends to vanish when the same ritual enters *The Rape,* for what is occurring in the poetic version is the inference of partial autonomy for the objects under view, blurring the issue of who or what is in control. It is the berries which crackle, the mill which turns round. Liquors which, by transferred epithet, can be described as grateful, glide, while the cups, with equal stress on their performing abilities, both receive and prolong.

Parallel to this technique is the treatment of the Baron's actual assault upon Belinda, where Pope's resources in revitalising stock notions of poetic diction succeed in directing attention to the instrument itself with which the Baron carries out his designs. The "two-edged Weapon," the "little Engine," the "glitt'ring *Forfex*" and the "fatal Engine" all serve to maintain the sense of object predominance until the grammar suggests that the "Instruments of Ill," a pair of scissors, complete the assault on their own; "The meeting Points the Sacred Hair dissever / From the fair Head, for ever and for ever!" (3.153–54). Such examples provide instances of the ways in which the grammar of the poem carries this sustained pattern of meaning: inanimate noun phrases repeatedly cast in an agentive role, or human activity finding its strict equivalent in nonhuman activity ("Nymph shall break. . . . Jar [shall] receive," or, more ambiguously perhaps, "the nice Conduct of a *clouded Cane*"). And Belinda's own words indicate the extreme lengths to which this transfer of power has been carried: "Thrice from my trembling hand, the *Patch-box* fell; / The tott'ring *China* shook without a Wind" (4.153–54), where the first of these lines suggests wilful action on the part of the patch-box (it was not dropped, it fell), and the second, picking up an image which forms part of the total pattern, confronts us directly with the automatic drama of object-life.

III

It is this ambience which helps to explain Belinda's complaint at the end of the fourth canto. "Oh hadst thou, Cruel! been content to seize / Hairs less in sight, or any Hairs but these!" (4.175–76). In desperation, Belinda voices her preference for real, but concealed, as opposed to attenuated, but evident, rape. Her assaulted coiffure is in visible disarray; retrospectively, actual rape at least offers the protection of an invisible discomposure. For it is in this fourth canto that Pope enacts most fully the reification that is at the heart of the poem. The comic descent into the particular grotesquerie of this hell is carefully designed to tell the truth of the preceding cantos, to reveal nakedly what has hitherto been artfully suggested:

> Unnumber'd Throngs on ev'ry side are seen
> Of Bodies chang'd to various Forms by *Spleen*.
> Here living *Teapots* stand, one Arm held out,
> One bent; the Handle this, and that the Spout:
> A Pipkin there like *Homer's Tripod* walks;

Here sighs a Jar, and there a Goose-pye talks;
Men prove with Child, as pow'rful Fancy works,
And Maids turn'd Bottels, call aloud for Corks.
(4.47–54)

One hardly needs the benefit of a Freudian method to discern how the previously repressed and fetishised sexuality is now producing its own pantomime of perverted psychology. But again it is the mode of this production that is interesting. Earlier the world of objects has challenged human sway, threatening to displace it; here, at a deeper level of psychological force, the nonhuman assumes total control of once-human vessels. Objects perform their "danse macabre" at will.

And if it is true that in this fourth canto Pope is revealing more openly the underlying concerns of the poem as a whole, he is also revealing something of "the truth" about the origins of Belinda's coquettish nature, and in this respect J. G. A. Pocock makes an illuminating observation. "The personification of Credit as an inconstant female figure, it is startling to discover, is a device of Whig rather than Tory writers, and in particular of Defoe and Addison at the time when they were undergoing the assaults which Swift, in the *Examiner,* had launched against all forms of property except land as 'only what is transient or imaginary.' " Taking up one of the writers mentioned, it is doubly interesting that Dickson chose to include as a frontispiece to *The Financial Revolution* a lengthy excerpt from Addison's third *Spectator* paper, "The Bank of England: vision of 'Public Credit'; her friends and enemies." In a dream Addison sees in the great hall of the Bank of England "a beautiful Virgin seated on a Throne of gold. Her name (as they told me) was *Publick Credit* . . . with the Act of uniformity on the right Hand, and the Act of Toleration on the Left." The dreaming spectator sees heaps of bags of gold behind the throne, piled to the ceiling, and learns that the lady in question "could convert whatever she pleased into that precious Metal." However, at the approach of "Tyranny," "Anarchy," "Bigotry" and "Atheism," the virgin "fainted and died away." There are already connections between Pope's "Goddess with a discontented Air," and Addison's "troubled with Vapours." But then, in lines not included by Dickson, Addison goes on to describe further effects of this invasion:

> There was as great a change in the Hill of Money Bags, and the Heaps of Money; the former shrinking and falling into so many empty Bags, that I now would have found not above a tenth part of them had been filled with Money. The rest that took up the same Space and made the same Figure as the Bags that were really filled with Money, had been blown up with Air, and called

> into my Memory the Bags full of Wind, Which Homer tells us his Hero received as a present from Aeolus. The great heaps of Gold on either side the Throne now appeared to be only heaps of Paper, or like little piles of Notched Sticks, bound up together in bundles, like Bath Faggots.

Again the echoes are clear as Pope describes his own Goddess of Spleen:

> A wondrous Bag with both her Hands she binds,
> Like that where once *Ulysses* held the Winds;
> There she collects the Force of Female Lungs,
> Sighs, Sobs, and Passions, and the War of Tongues.
> (4.81–84)

Both writers are expressing kinds of transformation, and the source of Addison's imagery suggests a more immediately monetary correlative for the social and psychological mutations explored by Pope. The point at issue here is not whether Pope is actively satirising Addison's essay, but rather that revolutionary forms of finance become a literary subject for Addison in ways that show definite affinities with the methods employed by Pope for his own more ambivalent purposes.

It is perfectly fitting then, that as the farce returns to the by now splintering elegance of the mundane realm in the final canto, Pope should make his final addition to *The Rape of the Lock;* Clarissa's classic statement of Augustan "good sense." But the significance of this inclusion reaches further than the simple assertion that "Pope obviously agrees with Clarissa." Pope, after all, controls the shape of the whole poem, and he has earlier (3.127–30), placed Clarissa in the invidious position of having unwittingly provided the Baron with the weapon for his assault. More important, though is the fact that the net result of her calm reasoning is action which first ignores and then noisily contradicts what she has to say. It is a way of acknowledging that the world constructed in *The Rape* is one that has moved beyond the bounds of Augustan rationalism and can no longer be naturally contained by it, given that its characters themselves are unnaturally "contained." And the poetic heaven which provides the final resting place for Belinda's much-abused hair offers one of the last images of the human contained within the inanimate. "There Heroes' Wits are kept in pondrous Vases, / And Beaus' in *Snuff-boxes* and *Tweezer-cases*" (5.115–16). The pessimistic gloom that settled upon Pope in his later years might paradoxically be traced to the exhuberant perceptions playing beneath the surface of his mock epic. In his mid-twenties he felt able to end the poem with a celebration of the breadth of his poetic vision. Indeed, he still felt able to revel in the proclamation of his own "quick Poetic eyes" as the only possible container for this disjointed world. Since the deeper meaning of Belinda's personal and social life is an insight necessarily denied to her, the structure of the five cantos brings it into focus for us.

From Moving Toyshop to Cave of Spleen: The Depth of Satire in *The Rape of the Lock*

K. M. Quinsey

In *The Rape of the Lock* a young Alexander Pope has constructed a masterpiece of tightly knit imagery, which reveals itself more on each reading of the poem: central images which jump up and meet the eye are found to continue in almost every line, diverging to explore different ideas, then uniting again into a single striking picture. For the sources of his imagery Pope travels from the universal to the tiny, from sky-shaking thunderstorms, rolling planets, and the four elements, to bodkins, tweezer cases, and a lady's hair. Images occur within larger images to give the reader a feeling of looking into a magnifying glass or a deep lagoon; and in the ideas which grow through the poem there is a similar range and development. In the Epistle Dedicatory of 1714 Pope declares that *The Rape of the Lock* was "intended only to divert a few young ladies," seeming to confirm that it was but "a jest" to laugh together two quarrelling families; yet breathing through his couplets are deeper emotions and a broader social vision. The "little unguarded Follies" of Arabella and her sex become part of a searching psychological study of the contemporary coquette, which itself moves out into a depth of social criticism anticipating the satires to come; and almost from its beginning the poem is pervaded by growing hints of the chaos which will end *The Dunciad*.

In his address to Belinda in canto 1, Ariel's description of the four types of Rosicrucian spirits retains an epic grandeur in its framework, being structured on the four basic elements of creation: fire, water, earth, air.

From *Ariel* 11, no.2 (April 1980).

Here, however, these elements become the four humours which determine feminine behaviour patterns, the spirits being visual representations of different aspects of female nature.

> But know, ye Fair, a point conceal'd with art,
> The Sylphs and Gnomes are but a woman's heart.

"The Fair" returning to their first elements after death remind us of the portraits in "Moral Essay II: On the Characters of Women"; yet it is interesting that the spirits all seem to show different traits in Belinda herself—almost subconsciously, from this point, we cannot accept her as a mere caricature of a certain kind of woman but must see her as a more complicated person who contains elements of all women. The "fiery Termagants" who mount up in air foreshadow both the flame of Belinda's anger (with an ironical relationship to the fires of love) and the fate of her lock, blazing off to the stars. "Nymph" is used generally to refer to a young woman, Belinda included (she is also associated with water in canto 2); but the "Soft yielding Minds" are like those of the young maidens who are so easily distracted by the "moving toyshop" parade of beaus ensured by the sylphs:

> When *Florio* speaks, what Virgin could withstand,
> If gentle *Damon* did not squeeze her hand?
>
> (1.97–98)

With the hint of the downward-sinking Gnome, however, forshadowing Umbriel's trip to the Cave of Spleen (the source of Belinda's anger and, to a large extent, a comment on her psyche), we suspect her of prudery as well.

Pope's concentration is on the sylphs, rather than the other spirits, and on their service to coquetry, both in his social commentary and in this as the dominant trait of Belinda's outward self. The attention is well merited, since the sylphs contain in themselves the basic paradox of Belinda's personality: although they "sport and flutter" like a modern-day "tease," they are essentially devoted to chastity, a duty which ironically relates them to their elemental opposites, the Gnomes. In the same way, Belinda's fluttery, sylphlike exterior hides a positively gnomelike psyche (as hinted in the Cave of Spleen). This relationship would apply to most coquettes, whose habit it is to flirt and vacillate, never making a true commitment to a love relationship. The sylphs are indeed the chief proponents of this inconsistency as well as being its visual embodiment—an impression particularly noticeable in the description in canto 2 of their "airy Garments" dipped in "ever-mingling Dies" of "Colours that change whene'er they wave their Wings," and in their constant movement. Yet from Ariel's opening revelation of sylphish duties we can see interesting parallels between she who "fair and chaste / Rejects Mankind" and those "predestin'd to the Gnomes' Embrace":

> Some Nymphs there are, too conscious of their Face,
> For Life predestin'd to the Gnomes' Embrace.
> These swell their Prospects and exalt their Pride,
> When Offers are disdain'd and Love deny'd.
> (1.79–82)

"Face" here can mean both physical beauty and reputation (a dual meaning developed throughout the poem); yet the preservation of both of these is a prime requirement of coquetry and the chief function of the sylphs. Both in worshipping her own image at the toilette and in her splenetic rage at the rape Belinda may be seen as being "too conscious" of her "Face"; and her prospects and pride are exalted both in the toilette and in the card game, as she "swells her Breast with Conquests yet to come." The "gay Ideas" of peers, Dukes, and the trappings of social status are gnomish dangers, Ariel warns, which "early taint the Female Soul"—yet this image itself looks ahead to the "moving Toyshop" contrived by the sylphs for maids' protection. In the metonymic effect of both "gay Ideas" and "moving Toyshop" we can see that there is but a short step from here to the Cave of Spleen: there, the posturing teapots and frustrated bottles make an implicit comment on the psychology of the Toyshop which sees a man as nothing more than his wig or his Garter.

The description of Belinda at the beginning of canto 2 subtly continues the theme of the "moving Toyshop"—in her "quick" and "unfix'd" mind and eyes we can see the activity of the "giddy Circle" of maidens' sylph-inspired affections, while at the same time:

> Bright as the Sun, her Eyes the Gazers strike,
> And, like the Sun, they shine on all alike.
> (2.13–14)

While emphasizing her centrality and divine beauty, this couplet also indicates a kind of superficiality, a lack of commitment to any one admirer:

> Favours to none, to all she Smiles extends,
> Oft she rejects, but never once offends.
> (2.11–12)

As Hugo Reichard points out, this impartial flirtation is correct behaviour for a successful coquette; in it there is a kind of balance or propriety, yet the rejection can easily develop into the "Offers . . . disdain'd, and Love deny'd" by the Prude destined to the Gnomes' embrace.

In this vision of Belinda as the rising sun, we have a symbol of the coquettish ideal which it is the chief duty of the sylphs to promote; in actuality, however, this brightness is but an imitation of the sun, just as the glitter of the sylph world is opposed to the warm fires of human love and sexuality throughout the poem. This opposition is apparent from Ariel's first appearance as "a Youth more glittering than a *Birth-night* beau," which contrasts to Belinda's own natural blush of excitement (all the more uncalculated because she is asleep).

The battle between the coquettish ideal and normal humanity occurs both on the social level and in Belinda's own psychology, and the sylph world, as described in canto 2, forms a good visual framework for it. In her efforts to "call forth" her beauty (with the aid of the sylphs) so as to rival the sun, Belinda is striving for an ideal that is as unnatural to humans as the "Field of purest Aether" in which the sprites enjoy the true "Blaze of Day" (2.77–78). The downward movement of the passage which follows these lines prepares us for what Belinda really is:

> Some less refin'd, beneath the Moon's pale Light
> Pursue the Stars that shoot athwart the Night,
> Or suck the Mists in grosser Air below,
> Or dip their Pinions in the painted Bow,
> Or brew fierce Tempests on the wintry Main,
> Or o'er the Glebe distill the kindly Rain.
> (2.81–87)

The only part of Belinda that comes near to rivalling the "Blaze of Day" is her flying lock, foreshadowed in the shooting stars pursued by sylphs; while the "grosser Air" and "Mists" look ahead to the climate of the Cave of Spleen, and the "fierce Tempests" to Belinda's temper and the war of the sexes which is brewing.

There are more hints of the "other" Belinda, of the "gnomishness" which naturally follows her sylphish aspirations, in the list of punishments with which Ariel threatens his troops in canto 2—"Gums and Pomatums," for example, the creams used to achieve a sylph-inspired beauty, are the exact opposite in their substance to a sylph's airiness. (In the "Characters of Women" the same contrast is devastatingly portrayed in "Sappho's greazy task.") We see also the "rivell'd Flower" of an aged beauty, and the vapours of Belinda's thoughts and of the Cave of Spleen.

With but a "sigh" as Ariel retires, Belinda is given to the dominion of Umbriel, who transports us to a full view of what underlies the coquettish exterior. This gnome can be seen both as an embodiment of her state of mind and as an aid to the action, exemplifying the dual function of the Machinery in the poem. In the Cave itself there is a similar ambiguity, which leaves us uncertain as to whether the Gnome is descending into a representation of Belinda's actual subconscious, or into a mythical underworld which represents what she *could* become. The description of the Cave contrasts to the sun and breezes of the sylph's realm, as it is "sheltr'd close from Air"; yet it reminds us of the artificiality which the sylphs promote as they keep us "imprison'd Essences" from exhaling. We can see in the hallucinatory images of Hades echoes of the punishments of the sylphs: "Lakes of liquid Gold" and "Angels in Machines." The "Vapour" in which Umbriel arrives and which hangs over the scene is itself reminiscent of the vapours of coffee and thought in canto 3—in particular the "Ideas" of an "earthly Lover" which rise from Belinda's mind and send Ariel into retirement:

> Sudden he view'd, in spite of all her Art,
> An earthly Lover lurking at her Heart.
> (3.143–44)

Whether the "Lover" is an actual person or simply an image for Belinda's natural urge to love, he is opposed here to "all her art"—either the arts of makeup, or the arts of coquetry which must dissemble rather than admit to an earthly lover. In the quick transition at this moment of Ariel's discovery, it is apparent that the darkness of the gnomes' world follows coquetry as inevitably as night the day:

> For, that said moment, when the *Sylphs* withdrew,
> And *Ariel* weeping from *Belinda* flew,
> *Umbriel,* a dusky melancholy Spright
> . . . .
> Down to the central Earth, his proper scene,
> Repair'd to find the gloomy Cave of Spleen.
> (4.11–13, 15–16)

Through the sylph-inspired repression of an earthly lover (he likely remains hidden from herself as well as the world), Belinda is subject to Umbriel and the Goddess of Spleen. She is hopelessly human and earthbound; like Umbriel, her "proper scene" is closer to "central Earth."

In the scenery and inhabitants of the Cave we see incarnations of different elements of Belinda, what she is and what she may well become. The "ancient Maid" shows the fate of both chaste Coquettes and Prudes; in her parody of a nun, she continues the lack of respect for prayers with which Belinda subordinates her Bibles to her billet-doux, only now the once-admired bosom is filled with "Lampoons." This caricature looks back to the brilliant example of zeugma at the beginning of the canto, describing Belinda's "Rage, Resentment, and Despair" at the loss of her lock, with its swift succession of pictures all significant with reference to her. In the "ardent Lovers robb'd of all their Bliss" and the "Tyrants fierce" we can see the Baron and Belinda respectively; yet we are also reminded that "scornful Virgins" when they have survived "their Charms" become "ancient Ladies" who are refused kisses.

The "becoming Woe" of Affectation reminds us of Belinda in her "Sorrow's Pomp" in 1712; and although this has become "beauteous Grief" in 1714–17, "Her Eyes half-languishing, half-drown'd in Tears" give the impression that her grief is a little undecided and even insincere. Just as the sylphs help shift the clothes, changing a flounce or adding a furbelo, so Belinda's eyes cannot quite decide whether to languish or to drown in tears, as a suitable reaction to the crime. In the emphasis on appearance we can see how close the sylphs' functions come to the airs of Affectation, "Wrapt in a Gown, for Sickness, and for Show"; even their constant movement and inconsistency can be seen in "each new Night-Dress" giving a "New Disease."

In his appearance Umbriel is a sooty-winged "dusky melancholy Spright," whose function is the exact converse of that of the sylphs—"As ever sully'd the fair Face of Light" (i.e., Belinda). As he lists his achievements to the Goddess of Spleen, we see that, like those of the sylphs, they all have to do with appearance:

> But oh! If e'er thy *Gnome* could spoil a Grace,
> Or raise a Pimple on a beauteous Face,
> Like Citron-Waters Matrons' Cheeks inflame,
> Or change Complexions at a losing game.
>
> (4.67–70)

Both Umbriel and the Sylphs are concerned also with reputation, and seem to equate it with appearance: all of Umbriel's lines here are suggestive of both—inflaming Matrons' cheeks (as with alcohol), planting heads with "airy Horns," rumpling petticoats, and upsetting prudes' hairdos. (This last could be an oblique reference to Belinda and her recent loss.)

Through Umbriel's address Pope expands Belinda's problems to include "the Sex from Fifty to Fifteen," and show how Belinda's denial of her own darker side contributes to her downfall. "A Nymph there is which all thy Pow'r disdains" is Umbriel's accusation: in the balance, Belinda is neither sylph nor gnome, but human.

One of the most interesting relationships between the world of the sylphs and that of the gnomes occurs in the previously mentioned connection between the Cave of Spleen and the "moving Toyshop" of a maiden's heart. Just as a disease is governed by a night dress, or as "transient Breath" is all that underlies Woman's "beauteous Mold," so in the minds of young coquettes all that is important about their beaus are "Garters, Stars, and Coronets"—the competition in the Toyshop is between wigs and swordknots, both unnecessary articles of decoration. Pope emphasizes, however, that this view of their lovers is the result of an overall outlook on society—these women see themselves as equally shallow—by painting the women as objects, usually a jar or a vase.

This is brought to life in Belinda and the powerful extent of "China vase" imagery associated with her throughout the poem. In canto 2, the "beauteous Mold" is transformed into a "painted Vessel"—it is left up to us either to look at Belinda as the gorgeous battleship decked out in Beauty's arms (she merges with the boat in our minds as Pope does not define the "painted Vessel" clearly) or to take the broader interpretation, the idea of woman as a container, empty (in this case) but beautiful. Like most images in the poem, this one bears a strong relationship to the underlying sexual discussion, particularly with later reference to the "frail China jar" receiving a "flaw"—a traditional representation of the loss of virginity. After the actual catastrophe, however, Pope shows the emptiness of his vessel Belinda, now "fall'n from high" to "painted Fragments"; he points here to the destruction of her splendid but vain shell of beauty, and also to her eventual fate as a mere human being—dust to "glittring Dust." The sexual significance of the empty vessel which should be filled, either by the sexual act or by childbearing, becomes even clearer when we look into Belinda's "toyshop" in the Cave of Spleen. Here Pope again brings to its point the recurrent image of people transformed to objects, giving us a beautiful portrait of the world as Belinda sees it and of the deeper psychology behind her view. Men and Maids here both resemble and have the same importance as the objects in her cluttered dressing table, which delineates her whole world: she can have no conception of them as anything more complicated than a jar or a bottle. Without Freud's help, Pope hints quite intimately at the problems of a "good" coquette—the thwarted sexual yearnings of the "Maids turn'd Bottels" and the sighing Jar reminiscent of Belinda herself. As in the confusion of "Garters" and "Wigs," Pope indicates here the vanity and affectation in Belinda's society: the unnatural pose of the teapots is surely a reflection of how she has seen the men around her in their foppish postures—"One Arm held out, / One bent; the Handle this, and that the Spout."

Not only people, but also emotions and intangible ideals are imprisoned in object form in this dressing-table world of Belinda and her contemporaries—there is a natural progression from the wits of beaus in snuffboxes and tweezer cases to love itself being transformed into a dressing-table object: "Lovers' Hearts with Ends of Riband bound" (5.116, 118). This makes a complete development from the relative whimsy of the moving Toyshop, to the psychological sickness of the Cave of Spleen, to the vision of social sickness and despair in the "Lunar Sphere." The true emotion of love is seen in the form of a chaste love object such as a billet-doux, in which the "Wounds, Charms" and "Ardours" are only literary. Similarly, in the incongruity with which Ariel lists potential catastrophes (2.105–10), "Honour" is equated with "new Broacade" and Belinda's heart is as easily lost as her necklace: intangible moral concepts and the seat of a person's emotions are reduced to the status of decorative objects.

On the level of the love discussion underlying the poem, the billet-doux is rivalled by the image of fire, representing human passions, which is particularly associated with the Baron. The shining and glitter that surround Belinda are like an imitation of the warm fires of human love and sexuality, just as a coquette's smiles are an imitation of true passion:

> When kind Occasion prompts their warm Desires,
> When Musick softens, and when Dancing fires?
> (1.75–76)

Knowing our natures, Pope intends these softly glowing fire images to be more attractive to us than the static language of objects and the insubstantiality of the sylph world.

From his introduction, the ardent-eyed Baron's association with fire is apparent, as he raises with "am'rous Sighs" a fire more powerful than Belinda's imitation sun. Indeed, he is a step ahead of the sun (not to mention the sleeping Belinda) in imploring Heaven "ere *Phoebus* rose." It is notable that his altar is built of six vast French romances, which correspond to the merely literary love of the billet-doux, and which presumably will burn as well. As it turns out, the fire does conquer: the symbols of coquetry are consumed on the pyre, and Belinda's lock, the ultimate love object, catches fire as it shoots up into the sky.

Yet underneath the glitter of Belinda herself there lurks hints of fire: from the unconscious "glow" of her cheeks in canto 1 to the "rising Fires" of anger fanned by Thalestris. As Geoffrey Tillotson points out, the comparison of Belinda to the sun is continued in canto 3, as the declining "burning Ray" of line 20 looks ahead to the nymph who "Burns to encounter two . . . Knights of *Ombre.*" Here, however, she is not so much concerned with her shining image as with a human feeling of competitiveness, seen in her more "natural" reaction to the prospect of defeat—"At this, the Blood the Virgin's Cheek forsook." And in the vision of the Goddess of Spleen "screen'd in Shades from Day's detested Glare" we have a possible hint that inwardly Belinda is not quite content with her sun image. We can see, however, that in her what should be the creative fire of love has become (through the repression of "all her Art") the destructive fire of anger. Herein perhaps lies the answer to the question posed in Pope's invocation:

> Oh say what stranger Cause, yet unexplor'd
> Cou'd make a gentle *Belle* reject a *Lord*?
> In Tasks so bold, can little Men engage,
> And in soft Bosoms dwells such mighty Rage?
> (1.7–12)

The conflict between love and coquetry is also expressed by means of two opposing sets of rituals which help to hold the poem together: the Toilette and the Coffee Hour, and the Baron's propitiation of Heaven and rape of the lock. In the mock Mass of the dressing table, Belinda begins as the high Priestess robed in chaste white, a celibate devoted totally to her religion—and she ends in the armour of Beauty, rising "in all her Charms" to sally forth on the Thames as its guardian Goddess. Corresponding to the Priestess, however, is the Baron who has built his altar before Belinda has even awakened, and who worships not his own image, but chiefly Love and the "Pow'rs" which exist beyond those of Belinda and the sylphs. The clutter of offerings on his altar is similar to that on the dressing table; but the objects are consumed in the fires of love rather than being laid in the "mystic Order" of the instruments of vanity.

At the crucial moment in canto 3 the two religions come into confrontation. There is a feeling of extravagant ritual (similar to that of the toilette) in the "shining Altars," "silver Lamp," and "fiery Spirits" of the coffee hour, as the priestess/goddess sits in state, surrounded by her hovering attendants. But in a quick moment the roles are changed, as the Baron, Priest at the altar of Love, takes over the rites and the priestess becomes sacrificial victim: the impression of ritual being conveyed by the "tempting Grace" or deliberateness with which Clarissa offers the weapon, and the "rev'rence" with which he takes it. After a fleeting vision of Belinda as the archetypal sacrificial virgin, with the blades spread behind her neck, it is only fitting that one of the symbols of her vanity is sacrificed instead. At the same time there is an echo of the underlying theme of mortality in this reminder of those truly tragic virgins in whom the severing occurs at the neck. The fate of the sylph "cut . . . in twain" reminds us that like "Airy Substance," hair *does* grow again; yet it hints at a far more dire separation, that of soul from body, at the time when "All those Tresses shall be laid in Dust."

J. S. Cunningham comments on "the *beau-monde*'s tendency to deify its trivialities and exalt its social occasions into rites, while casually neglecting what ought to be sacred." This can be seen in the conventions and formulae by which Belinda's whole social existence is governed: the toilette, the coffee hour, the obligatory "visit" which acquires a religious importance:

> While *Visits* shall be paid on solemn Days,
> When numerous Wax-Lights in bright Order blaze.
> (3.168–69)

Pope emphasizes this aspect of Belinda's society with epic ritualistic formulae, as well as repeated references to "the Watch"; but he brings it sharply to a point in the following black lines:

> Mean while declining from the Noon of Day,
> The Sun obliquely shoots his burning Ray;
> The hungry Judges soon the Sentence sign,
> And Wretches hang that Jury-men may Dine.
> (3.19–22)

Here the same valuing of ritual is carried over into life and death existence. In 1712 the connection between the hungry judges and Belinda's cronies is clearer, as the Coffee Hour follows on the heels of the judges' and jurymen's dinnertime; in this Juvenalian passage Pope is emphasizing the visceral impulse under society's ritual. (The death of reputations of canto 3, line 16, too, may be compared to the death of the wretches—taking place at a word.) The implication of the structure of the passage, which parallels the "Long Labours of the Toilette" to the judges' workday is devastating—here Pope is pinioning the values which can subordinate the death of a husband to that of a lapdog, and is putting them in the context of society at large. Among others, Murray Kreiger in his article "The 'Frail China Jar' and the Rude Hand of Chaos" has interpreted this couplet as presenting an ugly alternative to Belinda's world, a world whose "fragile decorum" and "disinvolvement" from reality make it precious. It would seem by this passage, however, that Pope is suggesting rather that the world of the judges is an *extension* of Belinda's world; that the topsy-turvy values and lack of moral substance which constitute its "fragile decorum" have here become a mortally important force in the world of "justice." The coquette's lack of commitment, her refusal of the social responsibilities of love and wifehood, is paralleled by the judges' abdication of responsibility—both are inhumane.

This same sense of incongruity is more subtly expressed at many other points in the poem, such as Ariel's listing of the different duties of the sylphs in canto 2, which delicately hints at a sense of despair in that these incarnations of frivolity and impermanence guide all human actions, with special attentions to the British Throne. (Indeed, the same or related forces which control the "mystic Mazes" of women's whims [1.92] are those which guide the stars and planets.) Similarly, in his description of the Toilette in canto 2, Pope's ceremonial, world-encompassing language, like that of *The Dunciad,* book 4, gives a vision of the whole world offering itself at this altar to vanity:

> Unnumber'd Treasures ope at once, and here
> The various Off'rings of the World appear
> . . . .
> This Casket *India*'s glowing Gems unlocks,
> And all *Arabia* breathes from yonder Box.
> (1.129–30, 133–34)

Another epic convention, that of giving the pedigree of the hero's equipment, affords Pope an excellent opportunity for a condensed picture of social decline as he describes the ancestry of Belinda's "deadly Bodkin" in canto 5, lines 88–96; it had descended from the Lord Chancellor's chain, to a belt buckle for his widow, to a baby's whistle, and finally to its present hair-gracing state. The poet manages to compress into this image not only the vision of a civilisation decaying into triviality but also a sense of its scrambled priorities and possibly of female responsibility—a sense which is even stronger in canto 2, as the poet expatiates on the significance of the sacred locks:

> Love in these Labyrinths his Slaves detains,
> And mighty Hearts are held in slender Chains,
> With hairy Springes we the Birds betray.
> Slight Lines of Hair surprize the Finny Prey.
> Fair Tresses Man's Imperial Race insnare,
> And Beauty draws us with a single Hair.
>
> (2.23–28)

Mankind is ensnared by the tiny, just as the fish and the birds are, and it is this work of the sylphs which has a whole civilisation tangled in its web, an idea supported by the recurring image of hair as a prime weapon of vanity. Belinda's locks are nourished "to the Destruction of Mankind," and are graced by the same "deadly Bodkin" that her mother wore. In the line "And mighty Hearts are held in slender Chains" we have the same sense of greatness, of deep human emotions, bound by the tiny that is to be found in the "lunar Sphere" (2.18). And the compelling "Beauty draws us with a single Hair" contains the same admission as "Look on her Face, and you'll forget 'em all" (2.18). Although delivered in a lightly complimentary tone, this last line becomes more significant when we consider the replacement of the word "forgive" of 1712 with "forget"—there is now a hint that the mental erasing of Belinda's faults is not a conscious decision, that the moral awareness implicit in the word "forgive" has been dulled.

At the end of canto 5, however, Pope drops all his humorous and lighter shades of meaning to concentrate into a few vivid images his vision of the elements of society. Even the order in which he relates them, moving from heroic human achievement to the insect level, give us a feeling of decline—social, moral and intellectual—sharper than at any other point in the poem; and for me this is perhaps its moment of deepest feeling:

> Some thought it [the Lock] mounted to the Lunar Sphere,
> Since all things lost on Earth are treasur'd there,
> There Heroes' Wits are kept in pondrous Vases,
> And Beaus' in *Snuff-Boxes* and *Tweezer-Cases*.
> There broken Vows, and Death-bed Alms are found,
> And Lovers' Hearts with Ends of Riband bound;
> The Courtier's Promises, and Sick Man's Pray'rs,
> The Smiles of Harlots, and the Tears of Heirs,
> Cages for Gnats, and Chains to Yoak a Flea;
> Dry'd Butterflies, and Tomes of Casuistry.
>
> (5.113–22)

Here is a museum of triviality and tragedy, a collection of the symbols of the "moral chaos" of Belinda's society; it is the bleak conclusion of the theme of objectification, taken to the social and deep intellectual level. The wits of men are contained in objects reminiscent of the vanity of the "moving Toyshop"; and a Lover's Heart is no more than a billet-doux, tied round with a tag end of ribbon. Alongside these leftovers of Belinda's world, Pope vividly paints in a few phrases the hypocrisy at the base of this society—"the Smiles of Harlots," "the Tears of Heirs," and the pseudo-intellectual "Tomes of Casuistry"—and gives a black picture of what vanity and riches come to: "Dry'd Butterflies" (like the "rivell'd Flow'r" of an aged coquette) and "Death-bed Alms." In the emblems of hypocrisy we can see elements of Belinda herself, of the artificial nature of her smile and the insincerity of her tears.

The "Cages for Gnats, and Chains to Yoak a Flea" are the final instance of the theme of incongruity, here ridiculing false learning, but also reminiscent of the punishment of the sylphs and the incongruity of their tininess controlling mankind. In the following line, however, the satire goes deeper: "Casuistry" implying "specious reasoning about matters of conscience" even as "Honour" is equated by the sylphs with "Levity" in canto 1. It is defined by Geoffrey Tillotson as "the minutely argued adaptation of ethical rules" encouraged by the Counter-Reformation and portrayed by Pope in *The Dunciad* as one of the executioners of Morality; and Pope himself refers (in the letter of April 27, 1708, quoted by Tillotson) to the profound Casuists, grave Philosophers, who have written "whole Tomes and Voluminous Treatises about Nothing." The "Tomes" in this line, though physically heavy, have the moral and intellectual weight of "Dry'd Butterflies."

Here is an example of how the "Filagree-work" with which Pope's poem is crisscrossed carries in fact its own weight of meaning, a weight which is often to be found in its very lightness. One aspect of this meaning is evident in the idea of transience and mortality touched on previously; Belinda's beauty, for example, is shallow and brief, just as the "vernal Flow'rs" from which its colours are drawn are soon killed by the summer heat. When Pope draws out this flower symbol, the sense of impermanence soaks through the whole poem; Hampton Court, the seat of the government, is "crown'd with Flowers," Belinda wears a noegay on her breast (the beauty of the latter will hardly outlast its adornment), and even her conception of Christianity is confined to "Wreaths of Heav'nly Flowers." On the darker side of this image we have the sylph shrivelled up like a "rivell'd Flower," in a graphic picture of Belinda's future, and with his picture of Affectation Pope brings the flower image to its point: she combines "roses" in her cheeks with a hypocritical "sickly Mien," showing exactly what those roses are worth—they are associated with outward appearance, and only with youth, being "the Roses of Eighteen."

The "lightness" of *The Rape of the Lock* has even more weight when seen in the social context of an upset in values, as in the Lunar Sphere and the bodkin history—indeed it becomes the most powerful support of the work. Through this all-pervading idea of incongruity, of universal concepts reduced to trivialities and of tiny objects ludicrously exaggerated, Pope communicates his vision of a society whose priorities have become hopelessly scrambled as it descends into chaos. He even manages to convey a sense of decline through the order (or disorder) of his images, ending most often on an anticlimactic note: a striking example is in Thalestris's vision of universal destruction, once again involving the four elements of Creation:

> Sooner let Earth, Air, Sea to Chaos fall,
> Men, Monkies, Lap-dogs, Parrots perish all.
> (4.119–20)

This reflects the "moral chaos" which Williams sees in the couplet at the beginning of this speech:

> *Honour* forbid: at whose unrival'd Shrine
> Ease, Pleasure, Virtue, All, our Sex resign.
> (4.105–6)

Perhaps the most encompassing image in the poem is to be found in its very structure, in the shifts of mood which occur as Belinda's day progresses, preparing us for a climax not far removed from the vision of Thalestris. With hints of light and sound Pope manages to convey to us the onset of a great thunderstorm, deepening his ominous shadows under a brightness that grows thinner and thinner. Belinda's day starts at the sun's peak, noontime ("just at Twelve" [1.15]), and ends in storm and chaos. In canto 2 Pope ingeniously develops the sense of a "calm before the storm," of hints of doom weighing down a mood of peace, summed up best in line 50—"softened Sounds along the Water die." Although the "painted Vessel glides . . . secure," the sunbeams still tremble on the "floating Tydes"; the security is shifting, transient, mutable. (These hints will soon be borne out in the "trembling" sylphs of 2.142, and in the premonition of "impending Woe" by which Ariel is oppressed.)

Ironically, it is Belinda's narrowly won triumph in canto 2 which first touches off the storm; as her King "falls like Thunder on the prostrate *Ace*" she breaks the late afternoon calm with exulting shouts which themselves reverberate like thunder. Too soon, as the choric warning foretells, they will be changed to "screams of Horror" at the catastrophe of the rape. It is then that the storm breaks in earnest:

> Then flash'd the living Lightning from her Eyes,
> And Screams of Horror rend th'affrighted Skies.
> (3.155–56)

And it culminates in the chaotic battle of the sexes:

> To Arms, to Arms! the fierce Virago cries,
> And swift as Lightning to the Combate flies
> . . . .
> Heroes' and Heroines' Shouts confus'dly rise,
> And bass, and treble Voices strike the Skies.
> . . . .
> *Jove's* Thunder roars, Heav'n trembles all around;
> Blue *Neptune* storms, the bellowing Deeps resound.
> (5.37–38, 41–42, 49–50)

In the trip to the Cave of Spleen Pope has enlarged the darkness of Belinda's mind to include all women—"That single Act gives half the World the Spleen" (4.79)—and has centred in Belinda "the Force of Female Lungs," all the feminine ire of the world. And it follows that the results of this attitude, the war of the sexes (with its chaos increased to universal proportions by the mock-epic comparison to the gods) echoes from "the bellowing Deeps" to the skies; an entire civilisation loses its base and crumbles:

> Earth shakes her nodding Tow'rs, the Ground gives way,
> And the pale Ghosts start at the Flash of Day!
> (5.51–52)

There is also a tragic and magnifying echo in the reference to Othello at the end of the battle. Here the theme is similar—the overvaluing of a trivial object (the handkerchief)—and Othello's roarings end in a mental chaos comparable to that of the battle. This allusion brings to mind the idea of love betrayed or denied—"And when I love thee not, / Chaos is come again."

At the centre of the poem we find an example of an "extended image" in the card game, which draws neatly together the main images and themes of the work. It serves as a perfect expression of the depth of Belinda's emotion—if she "burns to encounter . . . Knights" it is only on the card table—but the game also carries the darker themes of mortality and social decline. In epic tradition, the images and action of the card game are prophetic of both the rape and the battle: we see Thalestris in the Baron's "warlike Amazon," and as Belinda is "just in the Jaws of ruin" there is a glimpse of the scissors spread behind her neck. Some minor images which thread the poem are continued too, in the Queens holding flowers, their emblems of "softer Pow'r," and in the pictures of the Kings: any sexual overtones in the King of Spades' "manly leg" are denied by his "many-coloured Robe" which hides the rest. And the "embroider'd *King* who shows but half his Face" gives us a sense of both hypocrisy and the decorative glitter of diamonds, reminiscent of Belinda's world.

As the various cards fall on tricks, their fate becomes heavy with a sense of mortality, in the mock-epic comment on the vanity of human wishes:

> Ev'n mighty *Pam* that Kings and Queens o'erthrew,
> And mow'd down Armies in the Fights of *Lu,*
> Sad chance of War! now, destitute of Aid,
> Falls undistinguish'd by the Victor *Spade*!
>
> (3.61–64)

The most striking effect of the game, however, is in its movement, which builds in speed and vividly portrays a society tumbling into chaos. The vision of overturned authority in the King of Clubs (he who normally carries the symbol of authority is now reduced to ridiculousness—"Giant Limbs in State unwieldy spread"—and his crown is of no avail) helps lead up to the climactic description of the fall into disorder. Here the glitter and vanity of the Diamonds, headed by the king of hypocrisy and his shining queen:

> Of broken Troops an easie Conquest find.
> *Clubs, Diamonds, Hearts,* in wild Disorder seen,
> With Throngs promiscuous strew the level Green.
>
> (3.78–80)

In the "Throngs promiscuous" there are overtones of the sexual discussion—the phrase reminds us of the coquette's lack of discrimination but connects it to a more serious and widespread moral disorder. Pope gives this fall worldwide reverberations with "*Asia's* Troops and *Africk's* Sable Sons," then neatly connects a vision of overwhelming catastrophe (like the onset of Dulness) with images of the cracked vessel and the divided hair:

> The pierc'd Battalions dis-united fall,
> In Heaps on Heaps; one Fate o'erwhelms them all.
> (3.85–86)

Perhaps the main importance of the card game in this discussion is as an image of the poem as a whole, as it portrays in miniature the same "orchestral combinations" of imagery and resulting richness of theme. The poem itself acts as does one of its images, expanding in a manner similar to the world it describes; as it moves from the light world of "jest" and literary entertainment to a depth and darkness of social vision, a deep humanity ties the two together. Just as there is both darkness and light in Belinda herself (and in her society), so the "light" mode of the poem contains both the incisive comment of the satires and hints of the broad vision of *The Dunciad;* our laughter at the "little unguarded Follies" of Belinda's world is always on the edge of a sense of the tragedy inherent in the situation as Pope saw it. Critics from Hazlitt to Tillotson have not known "whether to laugh or weep" over *The Rape of the Lock;* it seems possible to do both. Under the dazzling technical mastery of their depiction, both female follies and sweeping chaotic grandeur spring from a depth of feeling which assures our equally sincere feeling in reponse.

Truth and the Imagination: *The Rape of the Lock*

David Fairer

Lying behind *The Rape of the Lock* . . . is a long tradition of thought about the imagination, from Renaissance faculty psychology through to the empirical philosophy of Hobbes and Locke, whereby imagination and judgment serve different ends, one in the realm of beauty and "secondary qualities," the other in the real knowable world of "truth." According to this tradition, imagination is wayward, pleasure-loving, amoral, superficial and sets up false values; whereas judgment presents a truth which is stable and objectively known. Parallel with this philosophic tradition is the literary tradition. In the work of a handful of poets, Spenser, Jonson, Milton, Cowley, Rowe and Prior, we have seen how the distinction between imagination and judgment could be seen as a clash between beauty and truth, and how a cluster of imagery grew up around the figure of "Fancy," consisting of shifting colours, airiness, shape-changing and vanity: the chameleon and the rainbow.

In his final version of *The Rape of the Lock* (1717) Pope appears to sum up this tradition in a poem which shows how imagination is inevitably falsifying (either delightfully or distressingly so), a colouring which can distort the truth by blurring its outline and dimensions, and substituting the beautiful, though secondary, qualities from within our own minds. In *The Rape of the Lock* the truth presses its demands upon the imagination. The tension between these two elements lies behind the clash of personalities within the poem, making it at several levels a drama of the mind. Although the poem is not an allegory exactly, it is more allegorical in character than has usually been allowed. It is concerned with the imagination as a beautiful, amoral, irresponsible and alluring thing, a cluster of adjectives as apt for Belinda as for the sylphs, and it is by way of this parallel between heroine and mythology that I want to begin exploring the work's allegorical elements, and to offer an approach which can reconcile our appreciation of its imaginative world with an evaluation of its human concerns.

The most important feature of Pope's transformation of his poem from the two-canto version of 1712 to the extended five cantos of 1714 is the introduction of the machinery of the sylphs. It is generally agreed that as a result of their presence "Belinda's world is shot through with . . . exquisitely shimmering beauty," that they are brilliant, dazzling, and a triumphant exercise of the poet's artistic imagination. Nevertheless, John Dennis's accusation that the machinery does not affect the "action" of the poem raised the recurring question as to whether the sylphs are integrated into its structure. One way round this problem has been to detect in them certain symbolic qualities so that they relate to the social world over which they preside. Reuben Brower's list of what the sylphs "stand for" ("feminine honour, flirtation, courtship, the necessary rivalry of man and woman") risks overkill. Geoffrey Tillotson takes a more external, literary approach when he considers that the sylphs exemplify Le Bossu's prescription for the machinery of epic: "the sylphs are 'theological' (they represent 'good' and 'bad'), 'physical' (they roll planets and attend to the weather), and 'allegorical' or 'moral' (the machines include Spleen)." But the sylphs, being removed from the world of moral judgments, represent neither "good" nor "bad." They delight in beauty without judging it, being as concerned to protect earrings and fan as they are to preserve chastity. To them a "dire Disaster" is an aesthetic one, outraging decorum rather than morality:

> Whether the Nymph shall break *Diana*'s Law,
> Or some frail *China* Jar receive a Flaw,
> Or stain her Honour, or her new Brocade,
> Forget her Pray'rs, or miss a Masquerade.
> (2.105–8)

As with Keats's poetic imagination, which "has as much delight in conceiving an Iago as an Imogen" (Keats to Woodhouse, Oct. 27, 1818), so with the amoral sylphs. Neither are the sylphs physical beings: they are all light and colour, and Pope goes out of his way to stress their disembodied character as "Transparent Forms, too fine for mortal Sight" (2.61).

To understand the sylphs fully it is necessary to examine them in terms of the imagery we have seen as conventionally associated with the imagination. Pope himself is clearly aware of this tradition, since he repeatedly uses colour as the medium in which the imagination operates. "There sober Thought pursu'd th'amusing theme / Till Fancy colour'd it, and form'd a Dream" (Donne, *Satire 4*). (The thought is Pope's, not Donne's.) He can talk of love as "drest in Fancy's airy beam" (Horace, *Odes*), and describe how the imagination, in allegiance with the passions, can colour and misrepresent what a person sees:

> All Manners take a tincture from our own,
> Or come discolour'd thro' our Passions shown.
> Or Fancy's beam enlarges, multiplies,
> Contracts, inverts, and gives ten thousand dyes.
> (*Epistle to Cobham,* 25–28)

Pope regularly stresses the shifting, insubstantial quality of the imagination, "Where Beams of warm *Imagination* play, / The *Memory's* soft Figures melt away" (*Essay on Criticism,* 58–59). And as light is extinguished at the close of the four-book *Dunciad,* the fragile colours of fancy are the first victims of endless night: "Before her, *Fancy*'s gilded clouds decay, / And all its varying Rain-bows die away" (1743 *Dunciad,* 4.631–32). In this context it is necessary to quote again from a passage discussed [elsewhere], where Pope describes how tantalising a poet's imagination can be:

> We . . . do but labour to fall short of our first Imagination. The gay Colouring which Fancy gave to our Design at the first transient glance we had of it, goes off in the Execution; like those various Figures in the gilded Clouds, which while we gaze long upon, to seperate the Parts of each imaginary Image, the whole faints before the Eye, & decays into Confusion.
> (Pope–Cromwell, November 12, 1711)

What are the sylphs, then, but Pope's most powerful and sustained image for the imagination?

> Some to the Sun their Insect-Wings unfold,
> Waft on the Breeze, or sink in Clouds of Gold.
> Transparent Forms, too fine for mortal Sight,
> Their fluid Bodies half dissolv'd in Light.
> Loose to the Wind their airy Garments flew,
> Thin glitt'ring Textures of the filmy Dew;

> Dipt in the richest Tincture of the Skies,
> Where Light disports in ever-mingling Dies,
> While ev'ry Beam new transient Colours flings,
> Colours that change whene'er they wave their Wings.
> (2.59–68)

The imagery of rainbows, "airy Garments," glitter, tinted clouds, and every kind of "transient" colour, merges here into a brilliant insubstantial pageant. The vision will not hold still. The restless, dazzling charm of the imagination associates itself with Belinda, whose eyes as well as mind are "sprightly" and "unfix'd" (2.9–10), and it is this uncertain beam which sets itself up within the poem as the rival of the sun. To gaze in Belinda's face annihilates moral judgments.

Geoffrey Tillotson is in fact closer to the centre of the poem when he acknowledges the uncanny way in which it tends to demoralise the critic: "The criticism the poem provides is sometimes more a picture than a criticism. It is so elaborate, shifting, constellated, that the intellect is baffled and demoralised by the aesthetic sense and emotions." One of the main effects of Pope's introduction of the sylphs into his poem is indeed to give it this moral complication. Any censure of coquettish "levity" of heart is deflected onto the sylphs who "contrive it all" (1.104), and (working against Belinda this time) we withdraw our approval of female purity once we are told " 'Tis but their *Sylph,* the wise Celestials know, / Tho' *Honour* is the Word with Men below" (1.77–78). This kind of ethical alternative is obviously too clear-cut for such a work as *The Rape of the Lock.* Its moral subtlety goes deeper because it exploits the inherent ambiguity of the imagination itself, which enters the poem with the sylphs. They suspend our approval and our disapproval: "levity" and "honour" are concepts implying the operation of the judgment by "Men below" (in this context merely "erring Mortals" ironically "blind to Truth," however much they may agree on their evaluations). Such concepts are annihilated by the sylphs, who are "Spirits, freed from mortal Laws" (1.69), the masters of "Fancy's maze" whose skilfully manipulated distractions help to preserve the women they patronise: "Oft when the World imagine Women stray, / The *Sylphs* thro' mystick Mazes guide their Way" (1.91–92). Note the irresponsibility whereby the judgment of the world becomes a fancy, and the judging word "stray" is transformed to a delightful stroll.

An interesting comparison here, which illustrates how Pope handles the amorality of the sylphs, is provided by some lines from Henry Vaughan's poem "The Daughter of Herodias" which condemn Salome for perverting the seriousness of music:

> Vain, sinful art! who first did fit
> Thy lewd loathed *motions* unto *sounds,*
> And made grave *music* like wild *wit*
> Err in loose airs beyond her bounds?

The echo of this stanza in *The Rape of the Lock* reinforces the idea that Pope's sylphs, though they flirt beautifully with the sinful, are at the same time detached from it. The sylphs' fusion of music and movement, their "loose airs" are errant merely in terms of motion; they expose morality's favourite words (err, loose, wild, beyond bounds) as the metaphors of movement which they are. The ambiguous *vanity* and *art* of Belinda are rendered harmless through her association with the sylphs, who are *empty* and *decorative* as well as *proud* and *scheming*. Vaughan's adjective "sinful," however, glues the concepts together with a moral label ("Vain, sinful art!"), highlighting the way the sylphs, in contrast, loosen such words from their moral context.

In such ways the sylphs literally "demoralise," enacting the amoral role of the imagination by dissolving the tidy human boundaries between virtue and vice. In a threatening world, says Pope, girls are not guided by neat moral imperatives, but by their imaginations, and luckily for them, such a lack of human commitment is the very thing that preserves them. The imagination of the coquette offers so many distractions that she avoids falling victim to her admirers: the sylphs bombard women's hearts with images, leaving them delighted, distracted and uncommitted. "Fancy's maze" protects them, in that one image drives away another before things get too serious:

> With varying Vanities, from ev'ry Part,
> They shift the moving Toyshop of their Heart;
> Where Wigs with Wigs, with Sword-knots Sword-knots
> strive,
> Beaus banish Beaus, and Coaches Coaches drive.
> (1.99–102)

The eighteenth-century "toy shop" was "a fancy shop" and "toy" an "odd fancy" (Johnson). One toy shop at "The Three Rabbits, near Durham-Yard in the Strand" sold, among other trinkets: necklaces, ivory eggs, purses, garters, cane-strings, snuffboxes, counters for cards, combs, tassels for men's neckcloths, silver buckles, buttons, powder-boxes and puffs, and "all Sorts of Scissars"—in fact, most of the small objects which crowd into *The Rape of the Lock.*

Pope's machinery of imagination, naturally expressing itself in terms of shifting lights, finds a striking parallel in the decoration he lavished on his Twickenham grotto. One early visitor delighted in Pope's magical invention in such terms as might have been used of the sylphs:

> Mr *Pope*'s poetick Genius has introduced a kind of Machinery, which performs the same Part in the Grotto that supernal Powers and incorporeal Beings act in the heroick Species of Poetry: This is effected by disposing Plates of Looking glass in the obscure Parts of the Roof and Sides of the Cave, where a sufficient Force of Light is wanting to discover the Deception, while the other Parts, the Rills, Fountains, Flints, Pebbles &c. being duly illuminated, are so reflected by the various posited Mirrors, as, without exposing the Cause, every Object is multiplied, and its Position represented in a surprising Diversity.

This appears to enact Pope's description of "Fancy's beam," which "enlarges, multiplies, / Contracts, inverts, and gives ten thousand dyes." Pope's "poetick Genius" resides in the perfect union of his art and his imagination: the disposition and workmanship within the grotto are skilful, but the poet has created for the beholder a place of deceit where objects are perceived by the senses not as they really are, but as through the distorting, enhancing glass of the imagination. The "Machinery" of "incorporeal Beings" (described above) fulfils a role parallel to that of the sylphs in *The Rape of the Lock,* throwing varied and surprising angles of light on the objects within: the cause of the aura is hidden, but the effect is to represent the objects now transformed as if by the imagination of the beholder. Just as the sylphs enact the imagination in Pope's poem, surrounding Belinda with playful light effects (so that the object herself is won over from the world of Nature), so the beautiful deception of Pope's concealed art within the grotto substitutes fancy's beam for truth. William Mason made this very point in his poem *Musaeus* (1747), in which Milton compliments Pope on his grotto, only to be told by the poet in reply that the place merely recalls "the toys of thoughtless youth, / When flow'ry fiction held the place of truth; / When fancy rul'd."

The scene of Belinda at her dressing table is a ritual of the enhancement of Nature, in which the imagination cooperates once more with art. She presides at a sacrament of transformation:

> This Casket *India*'s glowing Gems unlocks,
> And all *Arabia* breathes from yonder Box.
> The Tortoise here and Elephant unite,
> Transform'd to *Combs,* the speckled and the white.
> (1.133–36)

The rites are those of narcissistic pride, and the heroine is clearly arming herself for battle, but the presence of the imagination in this passage should warn the reader against reciting the moral too solemnly. Modern critics are agreed that the values of Belinda's society are confused, and the line "Puffs, Powders, Patches, Bibles, Billet-doux" (1.138) is frequently quoted as symbolising this disarray. Geoffrey Tillotson and Maynard Mack agree that the line betrays a "moral disorder" in the heroine's social world, and this is certainly true. But at this moment of the poem the emphasis is perhaps less on "society" than on the particular *inner* world of the coquette. This world may outrage our moral preconceptions and strain decorum to breaking point, but the disorder is fundamentally an imaginative profusion, and during this scene Belinda is becoming a creature of the imagination. For the moment ethical judgments are suspended, and the disarray is not "sad" (a critic's word), but delightful.

The necessary gloss to this passage is provided by Pope himself, in an anonymous letter contributed to *The Guardian,* no. 106, a few months before he completed the extended version of *The Rape of the Lock.* Its parallels with the poem are remarkable. In his dream Pope peers through the window in his mistress's breast and tries to sketch the confusion within her heart as one image rapidly chases out another: "The first Images I discovered in it were Fans, Silks, Ribbonds, Laces, and many other Gewgaws, which lay so thick together, that the whole Heart was nothing else but a Toyshop." Such disorder betrays the lack of hierarchy within the imagination. Pope is desperate to discover where he as a human being stands amongst all this female frippery, but he has to contend with some unexpected rivals for her attention. Her imagination turns restlessly from one image to another:

> There then followed a quick Succession of different Scenes. A Play-house, a Church, a Court, a Poppet-show, rose up one after another, till at last they all of them gave Place to a Pair of new Shoes, which kept footing in the Heart for a whole Hour. These were driven off at last by a Lap-dog, who was succeeded by a *Guiney* Pig, a Squirril and a Monky. I my self, to my no small Joy, brought up the Rear of these worthy Favourites. I was ravished at being so happily posted and in full Possession of the Heart: But . . . I found my Place taken up by an ill-bred awkward Puppy with a Mony-bag under each Arm.

Aurelia is plainly a coquette: the Church takes her fancy, but so does a pair of new shoes. Nothing is valued for longer than it occupies her imagination. Her image-making faculty is working overtime, but the judgment has no place. Amid this confusion Pope struggles to turn his own transient image into a permanent occupant of her heart. Similarly, in the poem the Baron's billet-doux, carrying its confession of love, is trapped amid the brilliant paraphernalia upon Belinda's dressing table, vainly asserting its message in competition with so many other rivals for her attention. To intrude a moral message about "the values of society" at this point risks blurring the fine suggestive detail that Pope achieves at the psychological level of his drama.

The product of the toilette is a new Belinda proudly displaying her hair to the world. The twin curls sported at her neck are not the result of judgment, but are created by the imagination as the coquette's chief weapon. They are there to entrap her male admirers in fancy's maze: "Love in these Labyrinths his Slaves detains, / And mighty Hearts are held in slender Chains" (2.23–24). The curl is literally a "fancy," since it is the sylphs (once again representing the imagination) who "divide the Hair" (1.146). After all, their duties in tending "the Fair" include

> To draw fresh Colours from the vernal Flow'rs,
> To steal from Rainbows ere they drop in Show'rs
> A brighter Wash; to curl their waving Hairs.
> (2.95–97)

The labours are not Betty's, but the sylphs' (though it is Betty who receives the praise "for Labours not her own"). At the dressing table art does all it can, but it is the imagination which presides and performs the decisive act.

During these "sacred Rites of Pride" Belinda is confirmed as a girl dangerously reminiscent of Milton's fanciful Eve. In the first canto her slumbers bring a "Morning-Dream" as Ariel appears to whisper at her ear. The dream, like Eve's, is a warning of her imminent fall, but one which should also inform and reassure her—if its advice is heeded. Here at her toilette we are again meant to recall Eve and the moment when shortly after her creation she is so taken with her own beauty that she gazes at the "smooth watry image" (4.480) in the pool, a gesture which hints at her pride (here justifiable) and her want of that "higher intellectual" (9.483) which Adam is meant to provide. Belinda likewise is fascinated by her own image, in a cameo which suggests how her pride and fancifulness will lead her into danger: "A heav'nly Image in the Glass appears, / To that she bends, to that her Eyes she rears" (1.125–26).

Now transformed by the imagination, Belinda becomes its creature. Emphasis shifts from solid physical reality to the shifting and intangible, so that in this new context her identity (as a newly "painted Vessel") merges with that of the boat carrying her to Hampton:

> But now secure the painted Vessel glides,
> The Sun-beams trembling on the floating Tydes,
> While melting Musick steals upon the Sky,
> And soften'd Sounds along the Waters die.
> (2.47–50)

The definition of the scene dissolves ("melting," "soften'd"); the winds play gently around her and the whole picture slips into soft focus as the "secondary" qualities of sound and colour take over. We are meant of course to recall here the magic of Cleopatra's barge as described by Enobarbus. Shakespeare's heroine, another exploiter of the imagination, lay on her cloth of gold "O'er-picturing that Venus where we see / The fancy outwork nature" (2.2.200–201). The purple sails were "so perfumed that / The winds were love-sick with them," and to the sound of flutes boy-cupids stood beside her waving "divers-colour'd fans," so that "from the barge / A strange invisible perfume hits the sense."

Thanks to the sylphs' transformation of her, Belinda is no longer the lazy girl hammering the floor with her slipper, but now resembles a "goddess" in the powerful hold she has on the imaginations of those about her. Her function is well seen here in comparison with Swift, whose goddesses are clearly *not* celebrated by the imagination; they are regularly shattered by fact and reality, their abstract beauty dragged into a suicidal conjunction (and rhyme) with the concrete: "Proceeding on, the lovely Goddess / Unlaces next her Steel-Rib'd Bodice" ("A Beautiful Young Nymph Going to Bed," 23–24). The art lavished on Belinda at her dressing table is raised far above this kind of thing by the mock-heroic direction of the poem (the inverse of Swift's movement towards travesty) which transforms the scene to a magic ritual. The phrase "Repairs her Smiles" (1.141) in a Swiftian context would destroy her, but as part of the "mystic Order" the sting of the words is strangely lessened. Even the idea of "toil" (powerfully felt in the "Anguish, Toil, and Pain" of Corinna's daily self-assemblage) gains a fastidiousness in Pope's lines: "From each she nicely culls with curious Toil, / And decks the Goddess with the glitt'ring Spoil" (1.131–32).

Like the imagination itself Belinda is brilliant, unstable, alluring, and independent of morality. Her curls may be her chief glory, but another object identified with her, and which she has power to transform, is the cross upon her breast. Enacting the imagination's power, she metamorphoses it from the symbol of Christian *truth* into a thing of *beauty*—a brilliant extension of herself sparkling in sympathy with her. Won from its responsibility within the world of Nature, it now annihilates creeds, and, uniting men rather than dividing them, becomes an image "which *Jews* might kiss, and Infidels adore" (2.8). But in the gossipy world of the court where truth goes for nothing and reputations shatter in a moment (a world thriving on fiction and fancy) this "painted Vessel" is precarious. Cleanth Brooks has usefully noted the recurrent references to the "frail china jar" as an image of Belinda's *chastity*, "like the fine porcelain, something brittle, precious, useless, and easily broken." But the jar represents the heroine even more closely than this suggests, for the fate that threatens it haunts Belinda also. The shattering of this jar would destroy its charm for the imagination. It would no longer be a thing for contemplation, whose wholeness and perfection lift it above a physical existence, but instead a mere artifact, whose pieces betray the laborious effort put into its making, now exposed as "painted Fragments" (3.160). Once cracked it would suddenly revert to its physical origins, revealing the "important Hours" that went into its making and which are not necessary for its repair:

> White lead was sent us to repair
> Two brightest, brittlest earthly Things
> A Lady's Face, and China ware.
> (Swift, "The Progress of Beauty,"
> 50–52)

Once more Swift's goddess has to confront the nightmare: her face no longer casts a spell over her beholders, but has descended to the world of truth, where it is just another cracked object needing repair.

Long before Belinda is roused by the lapdog and the Baron's letter (cunningly tied around the dog's neck?), the Baron himself has been engaged in serious business. Besides seeking a rendezvous with Belinda, he has constructed a sacrificial altar to Love, on which he has offered his whole collection of female frippery gathered from former idols ("three Garters, half a Pair of Gloves" [2.39] etc—his masculine version of the coquette's sword-knots). He has to this point lived within the fickle imagination of the lover (the twelve romances out of which he constructs the altar are evidence enough of this), but he symbolically abjures his career as a sexual philanderer for the one supreme prize. All the trophies which his imagination has fed on are consumed by the flames. One vision now haunts him, that of Belinda and her lock of hair: "Th'Adventrous *Baron* the bright Locks admir'd, / He saw, he wish'd, and to the Prize aspir'd" (2.29–30).

One critic has considered the Baron to be an unsympathetic philanderer, a man for whom the lock is merely the greatest of all trophies which he wants to acquire in order to increase his renown in society. This harsh view is misleading, since it tends to ignore the extent to which the Baron's imagination has fallen a prey to Belinda—the "slender Chains" of her beauty hold him transfixed, and the coquette's own aggressiveness is stressed at several points. Nor should we forget the figure of the foppish Sir Plume who confronts him after the "rape"—the Baron's dignified and self-possessed reply (4.131–40) shows the contrast between them, and his alliance with Clarissa also suggests that Pope does not see him as a mere "philanderer." No, his seizure of the lock is more the act of the adventurous lover as described by Spenser:

> [Her] image printing in his deepest wit,
> He thereon feeds his hungrie fantasy,
> Still full, yet never satisfyde with it
> . . . .
> Thereon his mynd affixed wholly is,
> Ne thinks on ought, but how it to attain;
> His care, his joy, his hope is all on this
> . . . .
> Then forth he casts in his unquiet thought,
> What he may do, her favour to obtaine;
> What brave exploit, what perill hardly wrought.
> (*An Hymne in Honour of Love,* 197–220)

The lock as we know is more than mere hair; it is the source of Belinda's power. It is up to the Baron, with Clarissa's help, to bring this goddess down to earth, to the solid ground where things stand and are known for what they really are.

In their encounter across the card table at Hampton Court Belinda plays the aggressive game of love, and, though the final victory is hers, she loses the Queen of Hearts to the Baron. During the interval of the coffee-drinking ritual he is given his chance to issue a public challenge to her feelings for him. The sylphs, aware that a "dire Event" is imminent, that Belinda's existence as a creature of the imagination is threatened, awake her consciousness of the cherished lock. But fancy's "mazy Ringlets" (2.139) are drawing the Baron inexorably closer:

> A thousand Wings, by turns, blow back the Hair,
> And thrice they twitch'd the Diamond in her Ear,
> Thrice she look'd back, and thrice the Foe drew near.

> Just in that instant, anxious *Ariel* sought
> The close Recesses of the Virgin's Thought;
> As on the Nosegay in her Breast reclin'd,
> He watch'd th'Ideas rising in her Mind,
> Sudden he view'd, in spite of all her Art,
> An Earthly Lover lurking at her Heart.
>
> (3.136–44)

We are reminded of the busy imagery of Aurelia's heart in the *Guardian* essay. Here Ariel, through Momus's glass, watches the "Ideas" within her, and he is disturbed by what he sees, because it threatens the *fancy-free* world in which Belinda has hitherto lived, and over which the sylphs preside. This is both the moment at which the virgin is to fall, and the moment when the imagination is challenged by truth. By loving the Baron (wearing his image in her heart) Belinda no longer "rejects Mankind" (1.68). Ariel does not abandon her out of pique but because the sylphs, who like Pope's imagination have worshipped and cherished her, are rendered powerless the moment truth intervenes. And so inevitably Ariel retires from her with a sigh, "his Pow'r expir'd" (3.145). The mutual love of the Baron and Belinda is, literally, a moment of truth—that is why Clarissa supports it. She gives the scissors to the Baron in order finally to recall her from the world of girlish fancy. Aubrey Williams is right in seeing here that Belinda has been given the opportunity to make her "Fall" a fortunate one.

The sylphs and their lock are satanically involved in the events of the poem: they tempt Belinda to wrongful pride and ambition, and they tempt the Baron also. The fact that Pope stresses the curling quality of the lock suggests that we are meant to sense its intriguing satanic character: Milton's devil hid within the "mazie foulds" (*Paradise Lost,* 9.161) of the serpent in order to lead Eve astray, and at the moment of temptation he appeared before her as a "Fould above fould a surging Maze" (9.499) as he "Curld many a wanton wreath in sight of *Eve,* / To lure her Eye" (9.517–18). We remember that Comus's domain is within "the blind mazes of this tangl'd Wood" (*Maske,* 180), a place where it is important that the lady see clearly, undazzled by the fertile imagination of her tempter. To sport with "the tangles of *Neaera's* hair" (*Lycidas,* 69) is to delight in the fanciful world of love elegy rather than attempt the true vision of the divine poet. Such Miltonic entanglements usually involve the delighted imagination, revelling in its "error" (a word whose etymology Milton consciously exploits). Nor is it only Milton who explores this idea:

The wanton lover in a curious strain
  Can praise his fairest fair;
And with quaint metaphors her curled hair
  Curl o're again.
(George Herbert, "Dulnesse," 5–8)

In "Jordan II" Herbert speaks of "Curling with metaphors" (the self-delighting imagination is distracted from Heavenly truth) and Crashaw describes how music "doth curle the aire / With flash of high-borne fancyes" ("Musicks Duell," 137–38). A sonnet from *The Phoenix Nest,* perhaps by Sir Walter Raleigh, provides an even closer parallel, when it speaks of "Those eies which set my fancie on a fire, / Those crisped haires, which hold my hart in chains." By linking Belinda's curls with the equally traditional idea of "fancy's maze" (and perhaps recalling a line of Cowley: "*Love* walks the pleasant Mazes of her Hair," "The Change," 2) Pope is able to exploit the delightful falsehood implicit in the imagination. In the fanciful world which the sylphs represent, the maze is a beneficent idea, and it is human truth which threatens—the "mystick Mazes" through which they guide young women are a protection against reality. But it is in the curls of Belinda's hair that the Miltonic idea has full force. The lock allures her worshippers by its "mazy Ringlets" (2.139) which

    graceful hung behind
In equal Curls, and well conspir'd to deck
With shining Ringlets the smooth Iv'ry Neck.
Love in these Labyrinths his Slaves detains.
(2.20–23)

The dangerous *conspiracy* is confirmed when Pope remarks that "Fair Tresses Man's Imperial Race insnare" (2.27). Once Clarissa's clear beam of truth strikes through, however, curls become irrelevant, a mere distraction from the unpalatable truth: "Curl'd or uncurl'd . . . Locks will turn to grey" (5.26). The curl is less a "thing" than a temporary posture. The sylphs preside over it because it is a fancy; hair is the true thing, the curl (as Herbert's lines demonstrate) is a *metaphor.* No wonder that once the sylphs have gone, the remaining lock loses its curl: "The Sister-Lock now sits uncouth, alone, / And in its Fellow's Fate foresees its own; / Uncurl'd it hangs" (4.171–73). The "poor Remnant" has surrendered its power as a thing of the imagination. The truth about hair is that time will turn it grey, and, however alluring, a curl is only a distracting temporary beauty.

The Baron's outrage is that he treats the lock as a thing rather than an idea. With the help of Clarissa's scissors (the scissors being to truth what the lock is to the imagination) the Baron snips off the hypnotising curls, badge of coquettry, and thus challenges Belinda to descend from the metaphorical to the realm of truth. He also challenges her *pride,* that passion which her imagination has fostered and cherished. The Baron's action and Clarissa's words combine in an attempt to make reality dawn upon Belinda. The Baron may be her foe, but Belinda should be grateful for the truth—even from her enemy:

> If once right Reason drives *that Cloud* [Pride] away,
> *Truth* breaks upon us with *resistless Day;*
> Trust not your self; but your Defects to know,
> Make use of ev'ry *Friend*—and ev'ry *Foe.*
> (*An Essay on Criticism,* 211–14)

The Baron's initiative is given theoretical support by his ally Clarissa, who steps forward as truth's representative to insist that reality cannot be held at bay for long: "Oh! if to dance all Night, and dress all Day, / Charm'd the Small-pox, or chas'd old Age away" (5.19–20). Clarissa knows that Belinda cannot exist as an object of the imagination forever. If Belinda is sensible she will preserve what her beauty has gained; she will surrender her merely hypnotic "charm" (the allure of the imagination) in favour of a deeper and more genuine "virtue" committed to, rather than denying, human values. While the sylphs embraced her she rejected mankind—that is, she cherished the imagination and shut out reality. Clarissa's scissors challenge her: the sharp cutting-edge of truth has met material hair, not angelic substance which can unite again. Ben Jonson expresses this same idea very trenchantly in his *Discoveries.* He is talking about the way the senses entangle the soul in error, and how the reason is able to deal with this: "by those Organs [of sense], the *Soule workes:* She is a perpetuall Agent, prompt and subtile; but often flexible, and erring; intangling her selfe like a Silke-worme: But her *Reason* is a weapon with two edges, and cuts through." Clarissa's "two-edg'd Weapon" (3.128) is therefore not just a humorous parody of the hero's sword, but the weapon of reason which cuts through the entanglements of imagination.

Belinda's chief error has been to mistake the aura for the reality, and therefore to lose the human scale of things. Her beauty has made her adored, but it has also fostered pride and selfishness, cutting her off from her fellowmen. Pope alerted us to this danger through Ariel's words in her dream: "Know farther yet; Whoever fair and chaste / Rejects Mankind, is by some

Sylph embrac'd" (1.67–68). To reject mankind is to ignore the truth about herself as a woman ("the flesh-and-blood creature . . . who marries, breeds, ages, and wears, has all sorts of dire consequences—and eventually dust and the grave"). The cutting of the lock is a sad moment (the sylphs leave her for ever), but it is also, as Clarissa points out, her moment of opportunity.

Clarissa's speech at the opening of canto 5, which Pope added in 1717 "to open more clearly the MORAL of the Poem" (Pope's note), is an exercise in worldly realism. It is bringing the truth home to a fanciful girl, and so its tactics are common sense, good humour, and the knowingness and cunning born of experience. She acknowledges at once the power of beauty, but points out that without "good Sense" everything which this power gains will be lost. She therefore tries to turn Belinda's eyes away from surfaces to the moral qualities within (from her "Face" to her "Virtue," from "Charms" to "Merit"). Clarissa's practicality shows in the stress she places upon learning something useful, and in her determination to confront Belinda with "those foes to Fair ones, Time and Thought":

> But since, alas! frail Beauty must decay,
> Curl'd or uncurl'd, since Locks will turn to grey,
> Since painted, or not painted, al shall fade,
> And she who scorns a Man, must die a Maid;
> What then remains, but well our Pow'r to use,
> And keep good Humour still whate'er we lose?
> (5.25–30)

Clarissa's tone supports the contrast she is trying to make, between the superficial things of life and its stark realities. "Curl'd or uncurl'd," "painted, or not painted"—the phrases chime hesitatingly alongside the laconic factual sentences ("Beauty must decay," "Locks will turn to grey," "all shall fade") which toll the truths Belinda must recognise.

J. S. Cunningham detects within Clarissa's speech some "limitations in her range of vision" (rightly, perhaps, since she is asserting truth, not imagination) and he is troubled by her worldliness and opportunism. But in this, as in other ways, Pope has judged his tone to perfection. Clarissa, expressing the moral of the poem, must obviously be cleared of any hint of prudishness: indeed, it is against this that she issues her warning. Her "opportunism" is in fact an attempt to recall imagination back to reality, and though she fails to persuade Belinda, her words reecho as we contemplate the heroine's fall.

The Baron acts, and Belinda reacts prudishly. In allegorical terms the gnome Umbriel (a prude roaming the earth in search of mischief) descends into Belinda's spleen to give her a "hypochondriack fit" or "the vapours," a fashionable disease for distraught young ladies. The spleen itself is technically the seedbed of the base imagination, the melancholy fancy which in woman can lead to self-delusions and hysteria. Bright's *Treatise of Melancholie* (1586) puts it pithily: "darknes & cloudes of melancholie vapours rising from that pudle of the splene [pollute] both the substance, and spirits of the brayne, [and cause] it, without externall occasion, to forge monstrous fictions, and terrible to the conceite . . ." The Cave of Spleen which Umbriel enters is therefore dark and misty, a place of grotesque hallucinations:

> A constant *Vapour* o'er the Palace flies;
> Strange Phantoms rising as the Mists arise;
> Dreadful, as Hermit's Dreams in haunted Shades,
> Or bright as Visions of expiring Maids.
>
> (4.39–42)

Umbriel, "a dusky melancholy Spright," feels at home here, for the human body is the element of earth, and gnomes sink downward by nature (1.63). If the sylphs inspire pleasurable dreams, then the gnomes bring the nightmares. Robert Burton describes this "hypochondriacal melancholy" in these terms: "windy vapours ascend up to the brain, which trouble the imagination, and cause fear, sorrow, dullness, heaviness, many terrible conceits and chimeras . . . and compel good, wise, honest, discreet men . . . to dote, speak and do that which becomes them not." And Thomas Walkington, in describing the dire effects of "adust melancholy," describes how the sufferers "are in bondage to many ridiculous passions": "Ther was one possest with this humour, that tooke a strong conceit, that he was changed into an earthen vessell, who earnestly intreated his friends in any case not to come neare him." This nightmare breaks in upon the now distraught Belinda. Pope's version of the unpleasant melancholy fancies which haunt her is a playful one:

> Unnumber'd Throngs on ev'ry side are seen
> Of Bodies chang'd to various Forms by *Spleen*.
> Here living *Teapots* stand, one Arm held out,
> One bent; the Handle this, and that the Spout
>
> . . . .
>
> Men prove with Child, as pow'rful Fancy works,
> And Maids turn'd Bottels, call aloud for Corks.
>
> (4.47–54)

The transforming "pow'rful Fancy" has become a nightmare of sexual incongruity. Vessels have merged with the human form once again, but no longer to recall a china vase or Cleopatra's barge. Here they gesture mockingly, and like Comus's grotesque followers these metamorphosed figures warn against the lure of physical desire.

Belinda's fanciful reaction to the "rape" takes the wrong, prudish form, failing to see the Baron's action as a social joke which relies for its deeper meaning on his dedication to his love. The joke-rape, nevertheless, is a perversion of what Belinda has been wanting, a gesture which to achieve womanhood she should have accepted calmly and rightly. The result of this inability to see clearly at the important moment is that Belinda turns at once from coquette to prude, from a flighty and irresponsible girl towards a possible bleak future as an old maid. Clarissa's prophecy (laughed out of the coquettish world that surrounds Belinda) has struck the mark. Maturity *must* finally dispel imagination, here taking the form of the brilliant mythological world of the sylphs and gnomes. Belinda has freed herself from the coquettish fancy of the sylphs, but only to be reclaimed by the imagination in the shape of Umbriel, who after his successful trip into her fancy-breeding spleen exults over his new disciple: "Triumphant *Umbriel* on a Sconce's Height / Clapt his glad Wings, and sate to view the Fight" (5.53–54). At the breaking of the gnome's vial Belinda yearns for a sad and solitary refuge:

> Oh had I rather un-admir'd remain'd
> In some lone Isle, or distant *Northern* Land
> . . . .
> There kept my Charms conceal'd from mortal Eye,
> Like Roses that in Desarts bloom and die.
> What mov'd my Mind with youthful Lords to rome?
> O had I stay'd, and said my Pray'rs at home!
>
> (4.153–60)

Such an overreaction is both false and fanciful, and is ominously reminiscent of Spleen's handmaid, *Ill-nature,*

> like an *ancient Maid,*
> Her wrinkled Form in *Black* and *White* array'd;
> With store of Pray'rs, for Mornings, Nights, and Noons,
> Her Hand is fill'd.
>
> (4.27–30)

It also echoes the longing for solitude in Adam's cry of guilty hopelessness after the Fall:

O might I here
In solitude live savage, in some glade
Obscur'd, where highest Woods impenetrable
To Starr or Sun-light, spread their umbrage broad.
(*Paradise Lost,* 9.1084–87)

The flattering sylphs have left her, to be replaced by the imaginative world of the guilt-ridden and prudish gnomes, the sad mental landscape of the melancholic. Umbriel's bag has its effect too, and as Thalestris "fans the rising Fire" (4.94) Belinda's mind forms a horrific picture of what had previously been a delightful ritual:

Was it for this you took such constant Care
The *Bodkin, comb,* and *Essence* to prepare;
For this your Locks in Paper-Durance bound,
For this with tort'ring Irons wreath'd around?
For this with Fillets strain'd your tender Head,
And bravely bore the double Loads of Lead?
(4.97–102)

The imagination has again transformed the scene, and for the lighter-than-air fancy of the sylphs has substituted ideas of oppressive weight and constriction. The act of imagination which created her lock is now seen (equally wrongly) as a ritual of bondage. The dressing table has become a torture chamber. Belinda cannot break out of her imagination, only migrate from one image to another. Clarissa, the truly mature woman (like Martha Blount in the *Epistle to a Lady*) is not enwrapped in the imagination in this way, but occupies an area within the poem set apart from the dazzling female world around the heroine. She stands before us on a pair of "sublunary legs" (in Keats's phrase), and her down-to-earth message, though it receives a chill reception, strikes the note of human truth.

But Clarissa's words are ignored as Belinda's world disintegrates into chaos and confusion. The lock, however, the cause of all this anarchy, has disappeared. Because all along it has been a fancy rather than a physical object, it is fitting that the lock should vanish during the struggle. It dissolves as all gestures of the imagination are bound to do. It would have "died" anyway once it had become separate from Belinda; it would have become a pathetic relic, telling of nothing but dust and ashes:

Dear dead women, with such hair, too—what's become
of all the gold
Used to hang and brush their bosoms? I feel chilly
and grown old.
(Browning, "A Toccata of Galuppi's," 44–45)

But Browning's cold draught of truth is not the note on which Pope wishes to end. The lock began as an object of imagination and now it is to end as one, playfully transformed to the most exalted level of vision. Pope ends the poem with a fancy of his own, by which the lock is awarded its final metamorphosis:

> But trust the Muse—she saw it upward rise,
> Tho' mark'd by none but quick Poetic Eyes
> . . . .
> A sudden Star, it shot thro' liquid Air,
> And drew behind a radiant *Trail of Hair.*
> (5.123–28)

By a delightful compliment Pope rescues the imagination from the chaos of melancholy and frustration on which the dramatic action of the poem ends, and makes a playful gesture towards its divine character. The stellification of the lock is a parody of the release of the contemplative soul as sought by Il Penseroso and the Lady in the *Maske,* to be achieved by the divine imagination's guiding the intellect to knowledge of God. The "quick Poetic Eyes" of imagination view the lock on its journey, and so do the sylphs who pursue it through the skies. In spite of truth's attack beauty has remained untouched, and, as with Pope's poem itself, the challenge to the imagination has brought about a glorious release. At the end of his work Pope suggests that the *Lock* will remain a vivid image for as long as men (whether beaux, lovers, stargazers or prophets) have imaginations. Arabella Fermor will now be the representative not of earthly, but of "Heavenly Beautie" like that celebrated by Spenser:

> By view whereof, it plainly may appeare,
> That still as every thing doth upward tend,
> And further is from earth, so still more cleare
> And faire it growes, till to his perfect end
> Of purest beautie, it at last ascend.
> (*An Hymne of Heavenly Beautie,* 43–47)

The Rape of the Lock explores so many aspects of the imagination: its kinship with beauty and pride; its opposition to judgment and truth; its insubstantiality, physicality, anarchy and self-deception; its functioning as dream, nightmare, madness and (finally) divine vision. The humorously transcendent ending, however, is a tactical flight from the challenge delivered to the imagination by the rest of the poem, and it is in this sense "detachable" where the ending of "Eloisa to Abelard" is not. Whereas the drama of that poem comes from the conflict between one image and another (enacting "the struggles of grace and nature, virtue and passion"), the drama of *The Rape of the Lock* pits image against reality, fancy against truth. "Eloisa to Abelard" is Neoplatonic in the way it presents the soul's encounter with the flesh, in its concern with different levels of vision, and its acceptance of the imagination as a path to divine truth. *The Rape of the Lock* can be seen contrastingly as an empiricist poem, with its opposition of imagination and reality, and its location of truth in the worldly, unillusioning good sense of Clarissa. The final stellification of Belinda's beauty is therefore best seen as a complimentary platonic postscript, flattering both to Arabella Fermor and to Pope's own art. By leaving his poem among the stars Pope certainly does not wish us to forget the many earthly issues which the story of Belinda's lock has raised. However, at this stage of his career he feels able to end in the realm of imagination rather than truth.

But Pope was soon given the opportunity to put matters in perspective. In November 1714 he discovered to his surprise that Arabella Fermor had married (not, incidentally, the "Baron"). In writing to congratulate her he completely avoided the fanciful compliment he had lavished on his Belinda. Approaching her now as a married woman about to take on many new responsibilities as friend, wife and parent, he stressed the "better things" that she could expect from her future status, "better" because these would be more firmly grounded: A poet's imagination had celebrated a girl's beauty and charm, but from now on Belinda the woman must strive for a more solid (though ironically less lasting) tribute:

> It may be expected perhaps, that one who has the title of Poet, should say something more polite on this occasion: But I am really more a well-wisher to your felicity, than a celebrater of your beauty. Besides, you are now a married woman, and in a way to be a great many better things than a fine Lady . . . You ought now to hear nothing but that, which was all you ever desired to hear (whatever others may have spoken to you) I mean *Truth*.

"Not with More Glories, in th' Etherial Plain"— "Slight Is the Subject . . ."

A. C. Büchmann

If allegory in general resembles a set of nesting boxes, where layer after layer symbolizes more and still more, then in the mock-heroic of *The Rape of the Lock* the ideal is displaced by small, mundane objects as the most capacious, outermost symbols. Belinda's lock, though merely a part of her, represents her whole person as well as itself; she may be an embodiment of vanity, but the symbolism is not commutative. Belinda does not represent her hair.

Pope's use of synecdoche is extreme to the point of personifying the implements of Belinda's life. The material objects approach the roles of allegorical figures when they incorporate their owners and take over the actions proper to the human, ostensible protagonists. Just as the "rape" is committed by the "glitt'ring *Forfex*" on the lock, not directly by the Baron on Belinda, so the preceding ceremonies, private and at Hampton Court, are carried out by combs, jars, spoons, and cups.

Throughout the poem, in an apt satire of materialism and snobbery, the objects crowd the humans increasingly. The synecdoche grows bolder, culminating in the human-object reversals of the Cave of Spleen. These reversals are less extreme than is often taken for granted; the objects which now behave more or less like people were half-animated before, and the people have been objectified and borderline grotesque all along. The people described are not necessarily further distorted than actual sufferers of the Spleen, the widespread English eighteenth-century malady: K. M. Quinsey points out that the gesture of

> living *Teapots* . . . one Arm held out,
> One bent; the Handle this, and that the Spout
> (4.49–50)

would have been recognized at the time as a courtier's affected posture. Conversely, according to Sir Richard Blackmore's contemporary *Treatise of the Spleen and Vapours: or, Hypocondriacal and Hysterical Affections,* delusions were traditionally considered a symptom of the spleen—"One has believed himself to be a Millet-Seed, another a Goose, or a Goose-Pye." The application to canto 4 is obvious:

> Men prove with Child, as pow'rful Fancy works,
> And Maids turn'd Bottels, call aloud for Corks.
> (4.53–54)

Pope's Cave of Spleen is inventive, controlled commentary rather than an interlude of sheer fantasy. The effect lies not so much in what he shows as in the frame he provides. He claims to be holding up a distorting mirror but shows actual grotesquerie, giving a proper frame to Belinda's world—an elegant reversal of the classical satirical maneuver of presenting a caricature while pretending that it is a naive report.

Prior to the severing of the lock, the world is shown as far prettier: the beauty of the material objects is united with the people, while after the cut the people and their possessions no longer correspond. The idyllic descriptions of the accoutrements can be taken as satire of materialism where the things are the better part of the people, as well as a parallel to *Paradise Lost,* where the human and the divine are separated; here it is the human and the material which before the "fall" are at one, so that "belongings" is an accurate word. The objects thus come to stand for spirit—nearly, not fully, or the volatility of mock-heroic would stabilize—while the humans are the flawed matter to which the less disappointing coffee cups and spoons temporarily are tied. In the long run, of course, the objects, not the people, achieve certain immortality: the lock sheds Belinda, whose symbol it was, and ascends to eternal life without her. The irony grows with the consideration that ephemerality has been a perennial basis for condemnations of attachment to material objects. Belinda, close to divine at the beginning of the poem, deteriorates more quickly than does the silver. That which generously could be interpreted as symbol of her beauty is revealed as all the beauty there is, and the glitter does not stand for equally shining virtues in their owners. The similarities to Swift's use of the rational faculty in *Gulliver's Travels* and of the clothes metaphor in *A Tale of a Tub,* point to the extent of Pope's satire in his synecdoches.

Emrys Jones has pointed out that mock-heroic was one of the few opportunities for serious Augustans to be both literary and playfully imaginative; he also mentions the "marked . . . aware[ness] of the high and the low in life as in literature" of Augustan culture. His emphasis is on the connection to the distortions of physical scale in *The Rape of the Lock* and *Gulliver's Travels,* but the play with moral standards is just as apparent: Pope conflates the material with what it stands for—

> On her white Breast a sparkling *Cross* she wore,
> Which *Jews* might kiss, and Infidels adore.
> (2.7–8)

Or else he conflates by mock-epic similes, where he keeps the original "high" values in sight by presenting them with duly high diction, then pulls the other end of the comparison up like a rope ladder after him:

> Not with more Glories, in th'Etherial Plain,
> The Sun first rises o'er the purpled Main,
> Than issuing forth, the Rival of his Beams
> Lanch'd on the Bosom of the Silver *Thames*.
> (2.1–4)

Or he compresses by synecdoche, another form of reduction which Pope uses to show delight as well. This last method, particularly, has the twofold effect of purging in alchemy: it reveals how great a proportion of the original substance is dross, but can also yield a pellet or two of pure gold.

> From silver Spouts the grateful Liquors glide,
> While *China*'s Earth receives the smoking Tyde.
> (3.109–10)

Pope catches glory in the very world he has reduced; such beauty or intensity are not to be had from a coffee party described whole. The synecdoche salvages and makes even more tangible the beauty in the tangible, and this triumphant and mischievous turn momentarily overcomes the limitations of the existence that calls forth satire.

Chronology

1688	Alexander Pope born in London on May 21, son of a Roman Catholic linen merchant and his second wife.
1696	Pope enters school in a seminary at Twyford and the following year is enrolled in Thomas Deane's school in London.
?1698	Pope's family moves to Binfield, in Windsor Forest.
1704	Friendship with Sir William Trumbull begins.
?1705	Pope suffers his first attack of the tubercular infection that will severely deform him. With a spine curved in two directions, he grew finally to only four and one-half feet. Headaches and a generally weak constitution plagued him for the rest of his life.
1705	Pope meets Wycherley, Walsh, and other London writers.
1709	The "Pastorals," Pope's first published poetry, appear in Tonson's *Poetical Miscellanies* (May).
ca. 1710	Friendship with John Caryll begins.
1711	*An Essay on Criticism* published in May. Pope meets Addison and his coffeehouse companions, as well as Martha and Teresa Blount, Gay, and Steele.
1712	The "Messiah" is published by Steele in *The Spectator.* The first version of *The Rape of the Lock* appears in Lintot's *Miscellany.* Pope becomes acquainted with a Tory group that includes Swift, Arbuthnot, Parnell, Gay, and Lord Oxford. Together they form the Martinus Scriblerus Club.
1713	*Windsor Forest* published. Pope is translating and seeking subscriptions for his *Iliad;* studies painting under Charles Jervas.
?1714	Meets Henry St. John, Viscount Bolingbroke.
1714	The revised five-canto *Rape of the Lock* appears.
1715	The first four books (volume 1) of *The Iliad* are published. Pope meets Lady Mary Wortley Montague.

1716	Second volume of *The Iliad.* Pope probably meets Lord Burlington.
1717	*Three Hours after Marriage* by Pope, Gay, and Arbuthnot, is performed at the Drury Lane Theatre. Publication of volume 3 of *The Iliad* and the first collected *Works,* including "Verses to the Memory of an Unfortunate Lady" and "Eloisa to Abelard."
?1719	Pope leases Twickenham on the Thames and moves there with his mother.
1720	The last two volumes of *The Iliad* published. Friendship with William Fortescue.
1721	"Epistle to Addison" and "Epistle to Lord Oxford" are published as prefaces to editions of Addison's *Works* and Parnell's *Works.*
1723	Pope's edition of the *Works* of John Sheffield, Duke of Buckinghamshire, is published but is immediately suppressed by the government because of the poet's alleged Jacobite sympathies.
1725	Pope's edition of Shakespeare (six volumes); volumes 1–3 of his translation of *The Odyssey.*
1726	The final two volumes of *The Odyssey.* Swift visits Pope at Twickenham. Friendship with Joseph Spence begins.
1727	The Pope-Swift *Miscellanies,* volumes 1 and 2.
1728	Last volume of *Miscellanies,* including *Peri Bathous; The Dunciad.*
1729	The Dunciad Variorum.
1731	The "Epistle to Burlington, Of Taste"—the first "Moral Essay" in a projected series on ethical issues.
1732	Pope-Swift *Miscellanies,* volume 4.
1733	"Epistle to Bathurst"; first *Imitation of Horace;* "Satire II. i: To Fortescue." *An Essay on Man* (Epistles 1–3) is published anonymously at the same time and enthusiastically praised. Pope's mother dies.
1734	"Epistle to Cobham"; Epistle of *An Essay on Man,* still anonymous; *Imitations of Horace* II.ii and I.ii.
1735	"Epistle to Arbuthnot," a tribute to Pope's dying friend; "To a Lady" (the last of the Moral Essays); volume 2 of collected *Works;* Curll's unauthorized edition of Pope's *Letters.*
1737	"Epistle II.ii," another Horatian satire; "Epistle II.i: To Augustus," which is aimed at George II; Pope publishes his own

edition of his *Letters* to replace the spurious collection. Authorship of *An Essay on Man* is now known; opponents of the poem's religious views launch an attack.

1738 Four satires: "Epistle I.vi: To Murray"; "Epistle I.i: To Bolingbroke"; "1738 (Epilogue to the Satires)"; Dialogues 1 and 2. Warburton, a clergyman, defends *An Essay on Man.*

1740 Pope meets Warburton.

1741 Pope publishes *Memoirs of Martinus Scriblerus* by various members of the club, and his correspondence with Swift. With Warburton's help, Pope revises *The Dunciad.*

1742 *The New Dunciad* (i.e., book 4).

1743 The final four-book version of *The Dunciad,* with Cibber replacing Theobald as "hero."

1744 Pope spends the last five months of his life revising his works for publication. The *Essay on Criticism, An Essay on Man,* and the four *Moral Essays* are completed and published before the poet, suffering from asthma and dropsy, dies at Twickenham on May 30.

Contributors

HAROLD BLOOM, Sterling Professor of the Humanities at Yale University, is the author of *The Anxiety of Influence, Poetry and Repression,* and many other volumes of literary criticism. His forthcoming study, *Freud: Transference and Authority,* attempts a full-scale reading of all of Freud's major writings. A MacArthur Prize Fellow, he is general editor of five series of literary criticism published by Chelsea House. During 1987–88, he served as Charles Eliot Norton Professor of Poetry at Harvard University.

MARTIN PRICE is Sterling Professor of English at Yale University. His books include *Swift's Rhetorical Art: A Study in Structure and Meaning, To the Palace of Wisdom: Studies in Order and Energy from Dryden to Blake,* and a number of edited volumes on literature of the seventeenth, eighteenth, and nineteenth centuries.

EMRYS JONES is Goldsmiths' Professor of English at Oxford University and the author of *The Origins of Shakespeare, Scenic Form in Shakespeare,* and *Towns and Cities.*

WILLIAM K. WIMSATT was Professor of English at Yale University. His books include *Hateful Contraries: Studies in Literature and Criticism* and *The Verbal Icon: Studies in the Meaning of Poetry.*

ROBIN GROVE is Senior Lecturer in English at the University of Melbourne. He has published on Emily Brontë and on Pope and is a member of the editorial staff of *The Critical Review.*

C. E. NICHOLSON is Lecturer in English Literature at the University of Edinburgh.

K. M. QUINSEY earned a doctorate from the University of London and has written on Alexander Pope.

David Fairer is Lecturer in English Literature at the University of Leeds.

A. C. Büchmann is a freelance critic living in New Haven who specializes in eighteenth-century studies.

Bibliography

Abbott, Edwin. *A Concordance to the Works of Alexander Pope*. New York: Appleton, 1875.

Adler, Jacob H. "Pope and the Rules of Prosody." *PMLA* 76 (1961): 218–26.

———. *The Reach of Art: A Study in the Prosody of Pope*. Gainesville: University of Florida Press, 1964.

Anderson, William S. "The Mock-Heroic Mode in Roman Satire and Alexander Pope." In *Satire in the Eighteenth Century*, edited by J. D. Browning, 198–213. New York: Garland, 1983.

Babb, Lawrence. "The Cave of Spleen." *Review of English Studies* 12 (1936): 165–76.

Barnard, John, ed. *Pope: The Critical Heritage*. London: Routledge & Kegan Paul, 1973.

Bayley, John. "Twickenham and Hampstead." *National and English Review* 134 (1950): 73–76.

Bedford, Emmett G., and Robert J. Dilligan, comps. *A Concordance to the Poems of Alexander Pope*. Detroit: Gale, 1974.

Berry, Francis. "Pope and the Verb Simple." In *Poets' Grammar: Person, Time and Mood in Poetry*, 120–24. London: Routledge & Kegan Paul, 1958.

Bluestone, Max. "The Suppressed Metaphor in Pope." *Essays in Criticism* 8 (1958): 347–54.

Bogue, Donald L. " 'Nature to Advantage drest': Pope and the Improvement of Nature." *Essays in Literature* 10 (1983): 169–81.

Boire, Gary A. "An Arrant Ramp and a Tomrigg: Pope's Belinda." *English Studies in Canada* 8 (1982): 9–22.

Brower, Reuben Arthur. "Am'rous Causes." In *Alexander Pope: The Poetry of Allusion*, 142–62. Oxford: Clarendon, 1959.

Brown, Laura. *Alexander Pope*. Oxford: Basil Blackwell, 1985.

Brown, Wallace Cable. *The Triumph of Form: A Study of the Later Masters of the Heroic Couplet*. Chapel Hill: University of North Carolina Press, 1948.

Brückmann, Patricia Laureen. "Pope's Shock and the Count of Gabalis." *English Language Notes* 1 (1964): 261–62.

Butt, John. "The Inspiration of Pope's Poetry." In *Essays in the Eighteenth Century Presented to David Nichol Smith*, edited by James Sutherland et al. Oxford: Oxford University Press, 1945.

Camden, Charles Carroll, ed. *Restoration and Eighteenth-Century Literature: Essays in Honor of Alan Dugald McKillop*. Chicago: University of Chicago Press, 1963.

Carnochan, W. B. "Pope's *Rape of the Lock*." *The Explicator* 22 (1964), item 45.

Clifford, James L., and Louis A. Landa, eds. *Pope and His Contemporaries: Essays Presented to George Sherburn*. Oxford: Clarendon, 1949.

Cohen, Murray. "Versions of the Lock: Readers of *The Rape of the Lock*." *ELH* 43 (1976): 53–73.

Cohen, Ralph. "Transformation in *The Rape of the Lock*." *Eighteenth-Century Studies* 3 (1969): 205–24.

Cope, Jackson I. "Shakerly Marmion and Pope's *Rape of the Lock*." *MLN* 72 (1957): 265–67.

Cunningham, William F., Jr. "The Narrators of *The Rape of the Lock*." In *Literary Studies: Essays in Memory of Francis A. Drumm,* edited by John H. Dorenkamp, 134–42. Worcester, Mass.: College of the Holy Cross, 1973.

Delany, Sheila. "Sex and Politics in Pope's *Rape of the Lock*." In *Weapons of Criticism: Marxism in America and the Literary Tradition,* edited by Norman Rudich, 173–90. Palo Alto: Ramparts Press, 1976.

Delasanta, Rodney. "Spleen and Wind in *The Rape of the Lock*." *College Literature* 10 (1983): 69–70.

Dixon, Peter. " 'Talking upon Paper': Pope and Eighteenth Century Conversation." *English Studies* 46 (1965): 36–44.

———, ed. *Writers and Their Background: Alexander Pope*. London: G. Bell & Sons, 1972.

Edwards, Michael. "A Meaning for Mock-Heroic." *Yearbook of English Studies* 15 (1985): 48–63.

Empson, William. *Some Versions of Pastoral*. New York: New Directions, 1960.

Fairer, David. *Pope's Imagination*. Manchester: Manchester University Press, 1984.

Folkenflik, Robert. "Metamorphosis in *The Rape of the Lock*." *Ariel* 5, no. 2 (1974): 27–36.

Freedman, William. "The Garden of Eden in *The Rape of the Lock*." *Renascence* 34 (1981): 34–40.

Frost, William. "*The Rape of the Lock* and Pope's Homer." *Modern Language Quarterly* 8 (1947): 342–54.

Fussell, Paul. *The Rhetorical World of Augustan Humanism: Ethics and Imagery from Swift to Burke*. Oxford: Clarendon, 1965.

Goldberg, S. L. "Integrity and Life in Pope's Poetry." In *Studies in the Eighteenth Century,* edited by R. F. Brissenden and J. C. Eade. Canberra: Australian National University Press, 1976.

Grenander, M. E. "Pope, Virgil, and Belinda's Star-Spangled Lock." *Modern Language Studies* 10, no. 1 (1979–80): 26–31.

Griffin, Dustin H. *Alexander Pope: The Poet in the Poems*. Princeton: Princeton University Press, 1978.

Guerinot, Joseph V., ed. *Pope: A Collection of Critical Essays*. Englewood Cliffs, N.J.: Prentice-Hall, 1972.

Hagstrum, Jean H. *The Sister Arts: The Tradition of Literary Pictorialism and English Poetry from Dryden to Gray*. Chicago: University of Chicago Press, 1958.

Halsband, Robert. The Rape of the Lock *and Its Illustrations 1714–1896*. Oxford: Clarendon, 1980.
Hunt, John Dixon, ed. *Pope:* The Rape of the Lock. London: Macmillan, 1969.
Jackson, Wallace. "The Word and the Desiring Self: *Rape of the Lock* and *Eloisa to Abelard*." In *Vision and Revision in Alexander Pope*, 39–66. Detroit: Wayne State University Press, 1983.
Jones, John A. *Pope's Couplet Art*. Athens: Ohio University Press, 1969.
Kernan, Alvin B. *The Plot of Satire*. New Haven: Yale University Press, 1965.
Klibansky, R., F. Saxl, E. Panofsky. *Saturn and Melancholy: Studies in Natural Philosophy, Religion, Art*. London: Nelson, 1964.
Krieger, Murray. "The 'Frail China Jar' and the Rude Hand of Chaos." *Centennial Review of Arts and Sciences* 5 (1961): 176–94.
Landa, Louis A. "Pope's Belinda, The (sic) General Emporie of the World, and the Wondrous Worm." *The South Atlantic Quarterly* 70 (1971): 215–35.
Loftis, John E. "Speech in *The Rape of the Lock*." *Neophilologus* 67 (1983): 149–59.
Lyman, Stanford. *The Seven Deadly Sins: Society and Evil*. New York: St. Martin's Press, 1978.
MacIntyre, Alasdair. "Epistemological Crises, Dramatic Narrative, and the Philosophy of Science." In *Paradigms and Revolutions: Appraisals and Applications of Thomas Kuhn's Philosophy of Science*, edited by Gary Cutting. Notre Dame: University of Notre Dame Press, 1980.
Mack, Maynard. *Essential Articles for the Study of Alexander Pope*. Hamden, Conn: The Shoe String Press, 1964.
———. "Humour, Wit, a Native Ease and Grace." In *Alexander Pope: A Life*, 239–57. New York: Norton, 1985.
———. *Pope: Recent Essays by Several Hands*. Hamden, Conn.: Archon Books, 1980.
———. "Wit and Poetry and Pope: Some Observations on His Images." In *Collected in Himself: Essays Critical, Biographical, and Bibliographical on Pope and Some of His Contemporaries*, 37–54. Newark: University of Delaware Press, 1982.
Manlove, C. N. "Change in *The Rape of the Lock*." *Durham University Journal* 76 (1983): 43–50.
Martindale, Charles. "Sense and Sensibility: The Child and the Man in *The Rape of the Lock*." *Modern Language Review* 7 (1983): 273–84.
Merrett, Robert James. "Death and Religion in *The Rape of the Lock*." *Mosaic* 15 (1982): 29–39.
Nelson, Timothy G. A. "*Double-Entendres* in the Card Game in Pope's *Rape of the Lock*." *Philological Quarterly* 59 (1980): 234–38.
Nicolson, Marjorie, and G. S. Rousseau. "*This Long Disease, My Life*." *Alexander Pope and the Sciences*. Princeton: Princeton University Press, 1968.
Nussbaum, Felicity A. " 'The Glory, Jest, and Riddle of the Town': Women in Pope's Poetry." In *The Brink of All We Hate: English Satires on Women 1660–1750*, 137–58. Lexington: University Press of Kentucky, 1984.
Nuttall, A. D. *A Common Sky: Philosophy and the Literary Imagination*. Los Angeles: University of California Press, 1974.
———. "Fishes in Trees." *Essays in Criticism* 24 (1974): 20–38.
Parkin, Rebecca Price. "Tension in Alexander Pope's Poetry." *University of Kansas City Review* 19 (1953): 169–73.

———. *The Poetic Workmanship of Alexander Pope*. Minneapolis: University of Minnesota Press, 1955.

Patey, Douglas L. " 'Love Deny'd': Pope and the Allegory of Despair." *Eighteenth-Century Studies* 20, no. 1 (1986): 34–55.

Paulson, Ronald. "Satire, Poetry, and Pope." In *English Satire: Papers Read at a Clark Library Seminar, January 15, 1972,* edited by Leland Henry Carlson and Ronald Paulson, 55–106. Los Angeles: William Andrews Clark Memorial Library, UCLA, 19.

Plowden, Geoffrey. *Pope on Classic Ground.* Athens: Ohio University Press, 1983.

Pohli, Carol Virginia. " 'The Point Where Sense and Dulness Meet': What Pope Knows about Knowing and about Women." *Eighteenth-Century Studies* 19 (1985–86): 206–34.

Pollak, Ellen. "Rereading *The Rape of the Lock:* Pope and the Paradox of Female Power." *Studies in Eighteenth-Century Culture* 10 (1981): 429–44.

Pope, Alexander. *The Rape of the Lock. An Heroi-Comical Poem in Five Cantos.* Illustrations by Aubrey Beardsley. New York: Dover Publications, 1968.

Preston, John. " 'Th'Informing Soul': Creative Irony in *The Rape of the Lock.*" *Durham University Journal* 58 (1966): 125–30.

Quennell, Peter. *Alexander Pope: The Education of Genius 1688–1728.* New York: Stein & Day, 1968.

Quintana, Ricardo. "*The Rape of the Lock* as a Comedy of Continuity." *Review of English Literature* 7, no. 2 (1966): 9–19.

Rawson, Claude, ed. *English Satire and the Satiric Tradition.* Oxford: Basil Blackwell, 1984.

Reichard, Hugo. "The Love Affair in Pope's *Rape of the Lock.*" *PMLA* 69 (1954): 887–902.

Rogers, Pat. *The Augustan Vision.* London: Weidenfeld & Nicolson, 1974.

———. "Wit and Grammar in *The Rape of the Lock.*" *Journal of English and Germanic Philology* 72 (1973): 17–31.

Rousseau, George S., ed. *Twentieth-Century Interpretations of The Rape of the Lock.* Englewood Cliffs, N.J.: Prentice-Hall, 1969.

Rudat, Wolfgang E. H. "Pope and the Classical Tradition: Allusive Technique in *The Rape of the Lock* and *The Dunciad.*" *Anglia* 100 (1982): 435–41.

———. "Pope's Coquettes and the Game of Ombre: *The Rape of the Lock* and Vergilian Exegesis." *Essays in Literature* 9 (1982): 251–60.

Scarboro, Donna. " 'Thy Own Importance Know': The Influence of *Le Comte de Gabalis* on *The Rape of the Lock.*" *Studies in Eighteenth-Century Culture* 14 (1985): 231–41.

Sena, John F. "Belinda's Hysteria: The Medical Context of *The Rape of the Lock.*" *Eighteenth Century Life* 5, no. 4 (1979): 29–42.

———. " 'The Wide Circumference Around': The Context of Belinda's Petticoat in *The Rape of the Lock.*" *Papers on English Language and Literature* 16 (1980): 260–67.

Sherburn, George. "Pope at Work." In *Essays on the Eighteenth Century Presented to David Nichol Smith in Honour of His 70th Birthday,* edited by James Sutherland et al. Oxford: Clarendon, 1945.

Sitwell, Edith. *Alexander Pope.* Harmondsworth, U.K.: Penguin, 1948.

Spacks, Patricia Meyer. *An Argument of Images: The Poetry of Alexander Pope*. Cambridge: Harvard University Press, 1971.
Tillotson, Geoffrey. *On the Poetry of Pope*. 2d ed. Oxford: Clarendon, 1950.
———. *Pope and Human Nature*. Oxford: Clarendon, 1958.
———, ed. *Augustan Studies*. London: Athlone, 1961.
———, ed. *The Rape of the Lock and Other Poems*. Twickenham Edition. New Haven: Yale University Press, 1940.
Wasserman, Earl R. "The Limits of Allusion in *The Rape of the Lock*." *Journal of English, and Germanic Philology* 65 (1966): 425–44.
Weinbrot, Howard D. "Masked Men and Satire and Pope: Toward a Historical Basis for the Eighteenth-Century Persona." *Eighteenth Century Studies* 16 (1983): 265–89.
Williams, Aubrey L. "The 'Fall' of China and *The Rape of the Lock*." *Philological Quarterly* 41 (1962): 412–25.
Wimsatt, William K., Jr. "The Augustan Mode in English Poetry." *ELH* 20 (1953): 1–14.
———. "Rhetoric and Poems: Alexander Pope." In *The Verbal Icon,* 169–85. Lexington: University of Kentucky Press, 1954.
———, ed. *Alexander Pope: Selected Poetry and Prose, 1688–1744*. New York: Holt, Rinehart & Winston, 1967.

Acknowledgments

"Patterns of Civility: Art and Morality" (originally entitled "Pope: Art and Morality") by Martin Price from *To the Palace of Wisdom: Studies in Order and Energy from Dryden to Blake* by Martin Price, © 1964 by Martin Price. Reprinted by permission.

"The Appeal of the Mock-Heroic: Pope and Dulness" (originally entitled "Pope and Dulness") by Emrys Jones from *Proceedings of the British Academy* 54 (1968), © by the British Academy. Reprinted by permission of the author and the British Academy.

"Belinda Ludens" by William K. Wimsatt from *Day of the Leopards: Essays in Defense of Poems* by William K. Wimsatt, © 1976 by Yale University. Reprinted by permission of Yale University Press.

"Uniting Airy Substance: *The Rape of the Lock* 1712–1736" by Robin Grove from *The Art of Alexander Pope,* edited by Howard Ershine-Hill and Anne Smith, © 1979 by Vision Press Ltd. Reprinted by permission of Vision Press Ltd. and Barnes & Noble Books, Totowa, New Jersey.

"A World of Artefacts: *The Rape of the Lock* as Social History" by C. E. Nicholson from *Literature and History* 5, no. 2 (Autumn 1979), © 1979 by Thames Polytechnic. Reprinted by permission.

"From Moving Toyshop to Cave of Spleen: The Depth of Satire in *The Rape of the Lock*" by K. M. Quinsey from *Ariel* 11, no. 2 (April 1980), © 1980 by the University of Calgary. Reprinted by permission of the Board of Governors, University of Calgary.

"Truth and the Imagination: *The Rape of the Lock*" by David Fairer from *Pope's Imagination* by David Fairer, © 1984 by David Fairer. Reprinted by permission of Manchester University Press.

" 'Not with More Glories, in th' Etherial Plain'—'Slight Is the Subject . . .' " by A. C. Büchmann, © 1988 by A. C. Büchmann. Published for the first time in this volume. Printed by permission.

Index